The Empty Book

Left: Josefina Vicens, writing *El libro vacío* and smoking a pipe
(ca. 1954–1958). Right: Josefina Vicens, 1988.

THE TEXAS PAN AMERICAN SERIES

THE EMPTY BOOK

A Novel

by Josefina Vicens

Letter of Preface by Octavio Paz

Translated by David Lauer

University of Texas Press, Austin

Copyright © 1992 by the University of Texas Press
All rights reserved
Printed in the United States of America

Originally published as *El libro vacío*
Copyright © 1958 by Josefina Vicens

First Edition, 1992

Requests for permission to reproduce material from this work should be sent to
Permissions, University of Texas Press, Box 7819, Austin, Texas 78713-7819.

♾ The paper used in this publication meets the minimum requirements of
American National Standard for Information Sciences—Permanence of Paper
for Printed Library Materials, ANSI Z39.48-1984.

The Texas Pan American Series is published with the assistance of a revolving
publication fund established by the Pan American Sulphur Company.

LIBRARY OF CONGRESS CATALOGING-IN-PUBLICATION DATA

Vicens, Josefina, 1911–
    [Libro vacío. English]
    The empty book : a novel / by Josefina Vicens ; letter of preface by Octavio
Paz ; translated by David Lauer. — 1st ed.
        p.   cm. — (The Texas Pan American series)
    Translation of: El libro vacío.
    ISBN 0-292-72066-1. — ISBN 0-292-72067-X (pbk.)
    I. Title.   II. Series.
PQ7297.V472L513   1992
863—dc20   91-25478
                                                                      CIP

To those who live in silence,
I dedicate these pages,
silently.

Contents

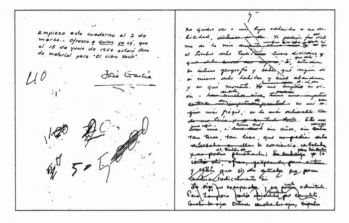

Opening pages of Josefina Vicens' original manuscript
for *El libro vacío*.

Translator's Acknowledgments

ANTE TODO, TE AGRADEZCO A TI, PEQUE, POR haber escrito este libro que dejaste en mis manos de traductor. I deeply appreciate the support of Aline Petterssen, whose solid commitment to the project from the very start has been indispensable; María Teresa Guerrero, who walks to the place where the fires converge; and my mother, Margaret Read Lauer, who has always been one step ahead and has taught me to open myself to other ways of seeing, thinking, and speaking.

I would like to recognize Mary Louise Pratt for her insightful comments and criticism, Jorge Ruffinelli for his suggestions, and Mary Jane DiPiero for her fine reader's eye.

I am grateful to the following people for making their documents available to me for my research: José María Fernández Unsaín, the president of SOGEM (La Sociedad General de Escritores Mexicanos); Guillermo Samperio, director of the Literature Section of INBA (Instituto Nacional de Bellas Artes); Lupita Soto, the curator of the INBA data base; Elena Urrutia, director of El Centro de Estudios de la Mujer at the Colegio de México; and Pilar Mondrujano at the Centro de Investigaciones Literarias UNAM (Universidad Nacional Autónoma de México).

I would also like to thank those who made it possible for me to study Josefina Vicens' cinematographic work: Lic. Ignacio Durán, director of IMCINE (Instituto Mexicano de Cinematografía); Juan Arturo Calva, assistant to the director of the

Cineteca Nacional; and Jaime Casillas from the STCC (Sindicato de Trabajadores de Cinematografía Corta), who granted me an illuminating interview.

I am indebted to Daniel González Dueñas and Alejandro Toledo for their excellent monograph about Josefina Vicens that was distilled from hours of taped interviews with her. I thank Sara Sefchovich, Carlos Monsiváis, María Luisa Puga, and all of those who allowed me to interview them about *The Empty Book* and Josefina Vicens.

I am also grateful for the institutional aid granted me in 1987 by Saint Lawrence University and for the financial support given me by the Andrew W. Mellon Foundation through the Center for Latin American Studies at Stanford University.

Introduction

MANY OF JOSEFINA VICENS' COUNTLESS ADVEN-
tures occurred under the signature of one of the several male
alter egos she created for herself. Probably no other writer since
the Portuguese poet Fernando Pessoa has consciously devel-
oped such a complex system of pseudonyms. "Pepe Faroles,"
"Diógenes García," "Alejandro Doncel," and "José García" all
allowed Vicens to float in and out of male arenas that would
otherwise have been off-limits to her. But she resisted eras-
ing her female identity completely because she often wrote
"Josefina" into her pseudonym by renaming herself "José" or
"Pepe," a variant of "José." Each alter ego had a separate ter-
ritory: Pepe Faroles wrote the bullfighting chronicles; Diógenes García authored political commentary; in the 1930s,
Alejandro Doncel expressed the anguish of Vicens' sexuality in
some fine, still-unpublished poems; and the frustrated writer,
José García, spoke of the author's struggle with writing. José
García, Vicens' last and most famous pseudonym, is a com-
posite of Pepe Faroles and Diógenes García. As "*farol*" means
"lamp" in Spanish and Diógenes is the bearer of light/truth,
Vicens stripped the light from these alter egos in creating the
clandestine novelist and author of *The Empty Book*, the gray,
anonymous José García, a Mexican version of John Smith.

Josefina Vicens speaks of one of her adventures in a revealing interview:

Interesting things would happen to me when I wrote bull-fighting chronicles using my pseudonym, Pepe Faroles. One day I wrote an unfavorable review of one of Arruza's bull-fights. Later, I heard that one of Arruza's friends, who happened to be a boxer, had promised to give 'Pepe Faroles' what he had coming to him. So I said, 'Well, that's all right, I'll wait for him right here in the office.' Alfredo Valdez offered to stick around so that he could protect me, but I refused. I had the boxer come in, chatted politely with him for a while and abruptly told him,

'Look, I have a pressing lunch engagement, so when are you going to get around to beating me up?'

He looked dumbfounded. 'But why would I beat you up?'

'Because I am Pepe Faroles.'

'Señora, *you* are Pepe Faroles?'

'Yes, *I* am Pepe Faroles, and you swore that you were going to beat me up, and now we've spent the whole hour chatting.'

'But, señora . . . No . . . How could I lay a hand on you? I—I just couldn't. It's been so nice to meet you.' [1]

Aside from its mischievous and subversive challenge to the gender system, this intricate labyrinth of pseudonyms reflects Josefina's obsession with the problem of identity. In *Los años falsos* (1982, published in English as *The False Years*, trans. Peter Earle [Pittsburgh: Latin American Literary Review Press, 1990]) Vicens forces the urban orphan, Luis Alfonso, to plunge deep into his own psyche in order to liberate himself from the shadow of his dead father. The father/son relationship becomes the point of departure for what develops into a fascinating commentary on contemporary Mexican political culture, patriarchy, and, as María Luisa Puga has pointed out, maternity. Vicens uses the *I* to challenge collective problems and employs masculine characters and discourses to dismantle the world they have created. The result is probably one of the most scathing criticisms of the Mexican political system ever written because it goes beyond superficial accusations and strikes deep into the origins of the system by destabilizing its mythic foundations. Even though Vicens claimed that the political theme was secondary to the problem of identity and adolescence, *Los años falsos* ties authoritarian political culture to the gender roles as defined within the family. Likewise, in *The Empty Book* (1958), Vicens' male writer-double, José García, wonders who he is as he uses language to plummet deep into himself. He prowls the streets of Mexico City in search of his place in a world that constantly empties itself of meaning. He scribbles in a nocturnal notebook in the belief that somehow the writing act can bestow meaning on his world. José García's experience mirrors that of the countless refugees of modernity who abandoned the countryside and flocked to the cities in order to survive.

Josefina Vicens' family came to Mexico City from Tabasco when she was very young. She was born in Villahermosa, Tabasco, on November 23, 1911. Her mother was from Tabasco and her father was Spanish, from a port called Soller in the Baleares Islands an hour away from Palma de Mallorca. He was brought to America at a young age, at about thirteen. He never knew his own country. Much later, the two of them traveled all over Spain because he wanted to see his homeland. Vicens had four sisters: Lourdes, the oldest, followed by Josefina, Amelia, Isabel, and Gloria. (Amelia and Isabel both died prior to 1984.)[2]

Vicens received little formal schooling because she left high school to learn secretarial skills at a professional school where she finished the two-year program in one year. At the age of fifteen she took her first administrative job, with the México-Puebla Transport Company. In one way or another she continued to be an administrator for the rest of her life, moving from one post to another following the dictates of opportunity and necessity. (When she died she was vice president of the General Society of Mexican Writers, SOGEM.) She began in a minor position in the Department of Agriculture.

"At the Department of Agriculture, they had this annoying bureaucratic habit; every morning when I arrived, I had to sign a huge roll of paper and put down my name and identification number along with the time of my arrival or departure. The daily repetition of my name got to be so unbearable that I started to change it. I put down my number and in the name column I'd write: 'Tolstoy,' 'Marie Antoinette,' 'Philip II,' 'Leon XIII,' 'Napoléon' . . . One day the chief administrator called me in and scolded me. I told him that the number was there to show that I had come at such and such a time and that that should be enough. He told me that I couldn't go on doing that, but I didn't give it any thought and went on with my list of great celebrities. Later, I discovered that the same bureaucrat would send for the roll when they had pulled it from the typewriter to see the name I had used. One day the head of the Agricultural Department sent for me; he was don Angel Posada, who was a representative and senator from Chihuahua, an honest man of complete integrity. (I did get to meet some honest bureaucrats and Ingeniero Posada was honesty with a capital *H*.) He said: 'You don't like to sign in, do you?' And I thought, 'Uh oh, now they're going to fire me.' I tried to stick up for myself and he interrupted, 'Well, you're not going to sign in anymore.' I told him that I had already figured that out and began to say my good-byes when he added, 'You're not going to sign in because you're staying right here with me as my personal secretary.'"[3]

Since her job at the Department of Agriculture afforded her a great deal of contact with farmers, Vicens soon became the head of Women's Programs (Acción Femenil) of the National

Farmer Confederation (CNC). She spent several years at this post before she joined Dr. Alfonso Millán to work at the mental hospital La Castañeda. Initially, Josefina was fascinated by the way many of the patients constructed their own characters and realities, but finally had to leave her job because she couldn't stand the despair of the more terrifying and hopeless cases.

After a short respite, Vicens entered the film industry and repeated her earlier success. She started out in a minor administrative position, over the course of the years became the president's secretary, and finally took over as president of the Short-Film Workers' Syndicate (STCC). She played a determining role in the revitalization of the film industry fueled by the Echeverría regime (1970–1976) as part of the cultural politics of "apertura" designed, in part, to legitimize the PRI (Institutional Revolutionary Party) in the aftermath of the bloody Tlatelolco massacre (1968). During this period Vicens presided over a genuine democratization of the script-writing process by dismantling the existing mafia and opening the doors to anyone who had a script or an idea for one. Scripts were read in a workshop, then the group made recommendations and submitted scripts for final approval. Many of them were purchased with monies that Josefina had acquired from the Echeverría government. Script quality improved significantly under her direction and Vicens deserves at least partial credit for the rejuvenation of Mexican film during that period.

Josefina's colleagues consistently recall her unwillingness to use her power to further her own ends. Jaime Casillas spoke of one occasion when she could have used her considerable influence with Rodolfo Echeverría, her immediate superior and also the president's brother, to obtain funding for her own script.[4] Vicens entered *Los perros de Dios* (*The Dogs of God*) in a national contest for script-writing in which the winner's script would be produced. The script took first place and Rudolfo Echeverría was completely surprised that Vicens' work had come to his desk by such a circuitous route. The official backing for her script, together with her status within the industry and the diluted censorship that accompanied the "apertura," enabled Vicens to work closely with the director, Francisco del Villar, so that *The Dogs of God* (1973)—a film which is now almost impossible to see—would still bear the mark of its creator.

In the film, Helena Rojo plays the role of a wealthy family's daughter who questions the existence of God and is fed up with the hypocrisy that surrounds her. She wonders how a God can exist who simultaneously threatens people with eternal damnation and forgives them through repentance. Repentance seems to her both an act of cowardice and hypocrisy. At night Helena Rojo abandons the sterile comfort of her upper-class home and joins her poor friend, played by Meche Carreño. Both Vicens' affinity with Rulfo and her work experience in the insane asylum come to life as her characters enter the cemetery. Helena indulges in her fantasies, most of which are sexual, by lying on the graves and creating roles which she forces her reluctant friend to play out. These improvised dialogues bring the dead to life for an instant as the young woman's fantasies become a spoken reality. When Meche's patience has reached the limit and the dialogues have exhausted themselves, the two young women take the freshest flowers from the tombs to resell on the city streets. Helena insists that her needy friend keep all the profits.

Many scenes evolve in symbol-laden dreamscapes typical of films from this period. Vicens' political side is apparent in one of the film's most charged scenes. The two women happen upon a night ritual in one of the working-class barrios. Under torchlight, the people begin to massacre hundreds of rats. Helena spontaneously joins the melee and beats several of the rodents to a bloody pulp. The mass of torch-bearing people, the low camera angle, and the use of rats to symbolize corrupt

government officials—a trope common to the Mexican political lexicon—come together to create a powerful political
image.

Of all of Vicens' films, *The Dogs of God* bears the author's
most distinguishable signature, expressing her preoccupation
with dual identities, gender and class, death, hypocrisy, the nature of transgression, and metaphysics. But, far from being a
facile, didactic film, *The Dogs of God* assembles an arsenal of
unanswered and, perhaps, unanswerable questions, ranging
from problems of class and sexual identity to the true nature of
sin and transgression. These questions make this film a daring
and provocative examination of the norms and conflicts that
forged the Mexico of the 1960s.

Josefina Vicens, "Peque" as she was known to her friends,
defined herself as a person committed to greater social justice
and became involved in those political matters that she deemed
important. During a conversation in 1984, she told me how
the U.S. Embassy had attempted to deny her a tourist visa because she had signed a petition protesting the CIA-engineered
coup in 1954 that overthrew the freely elected Arbenz government in Guatemala. When she denied having signed, the U.S.
official produced a copy of the petition bearing her name. She
cleverly answered that someone had obviously put her name
on the petition without her authorization. The official interro-
gated her further, asking whether she was a friend of Manuel
Alvarez Bravo, a noted Mexican photographer who had also
been blacklisted. She responded that of course she knew who
he was but had never known him personally. Since her plane
was due to leave in a couple of hours, the official finally issued
her a visa after extracting her promise that she would produce
evidence to support her claims when she returned. Vicens
boarded the plane with several letters in her purse that her
friend, Manuel Alvarez Bravo, had asked her to send to his
friends in the United States. When she returned to Mexico,

she not only didn't pass through the Embassy's gates but swore she would never go to the United States again.

Several years later, the situation in Guatemala would claim the life of her dear friend, Alaíde Foppa, the founder of the magazine *FEM*. During the rise of the nouveau roman, Foppa, along with Dominique Eluard, translated *The Empty Book* into French in 1963 (*Le Cahier clandestine*). Vicens spoke of Alaíde's unresolved disappearance in an interview: "When she was about to go to Guatemala for the last time, I remember that she called me up the day she was to leave and said, 'I'm going to Guatemala to see my mother. When I get back we'll have lunch and I'll tell you all about it.' Then, one day I was told that she had disappeared. It was horrible. Alaíde's case is different from all the others in my life because, as is only natural, many of my friends have died, but I've always seen them. Their death has been very painful for me, but I've seen them. Alaíde disappeared, and that was that. Certainly, beyond a shadow of doubt, the military government murdered her, but who's going to prove it for me? I don't know if she's rotting in some dungeon, whether they're still torturing her, or if she died a long time ago. She just vanished into thin air, no one ever saw her body. Alaíde had a very special place in my life, in my heart. Few deaths have affected me the way hers has."[5]

The Empty Book

YOUNG JOSÉ GARCÍA'S MEXICO HAD RECENTLY emerged from the first popular revolution of the twentieth century (1910–1917), the Cristero War (1926–1929), and the consolidation of the Institutional Revolutionary Party (PRI), all of which cost the country more than a million dead, massive social upheaval, and enormous material destruction. In the 1930s the definition of the national project was partly influenced by the social ideas of Luis Cabrera, Samuel Ramos' psychological profile of the Mexican, the educational system of José Vasconcelos, the novels of the Mexican Revolution, and Orozco's, Siqueiros', and Rivera's murals, the visual mortar of the official mythology. In addition to agrarian reform, the consolidation of a national banking system, the centralization of the Mexican Army, the creation of a national health system (El Seguro Social), and the nationalization of Mexican oil, Mexico embarked on an ill-fated, nationalistic project of industrialization.

José García's here and now is a rapidly growing Mexico City moving to the rhythm of mambos, rhumbas, and cha-cha-chas, a city filled with first-generation immigrants from the countryside, neon lights, and the new rumbling of gasoline engines. There are no televisions, but the radio divas seduce the public with tunes of the day. It is the moment of the expanding middle class that fills the bulging bureaucracies and the movie theaters in the heyday of Mexican film; the pace of change and the contradictions industrialization has produced are dizzying. *The Empty Book*, in this context, becomes a giant question mark generated by its relentless system of contradictions and its inability to provide answers. Carlos Fuentes' 1958 novel, *Where the Air Is Clear*, underlines many of the same points of conflict from the highground of omniscience. But such a totalizing gaze has no place in *The Empty Book* because Vicens shares her character's contradictions with the reader as more intimate, internalized reflections in the turbulent spirit of nonhero José García.

In 1958 very different novels emerged from the Latin American continent, among the most famous being *Deep Rivers* by

José María Arguedas, *Gabriela, Clove and Cinnamon* by Jorge Amado, and *Where the Air Is Clear* by Carlos Fuentes. The literary scene was fraught with debates between writers pitting "nationalist" against more "cosmopolitan" esthetics, with entanglements and maneuverings to see who would speak on behalf of very heterogeneous nations, and with battles to establish the most legitimate settings—rural themes versus urban. In Mexico, Rulfo's simultaneously rural and cosmopolitan masterpieces had brought down the curtain on the novel of the Mexican revolution and left a literary void. Although one can debate whether or not *The Empty Book* filled that void by signaling a shift in direction, Vicens' self-referential novel is undeniably the first work within Mexico to use narrative to debate the nature of the narrative itself.

In 1958, there were many who lauded Vicens' novel for having broken with the past. Today, most Mexican writers and critics hold some opinion about *The Empty Book* and recognize its importance. Marta Robles places the work clearly within the tradition of the existentialist novel and underlines Josefina Vicens' creation of a nonhero incapable of both noble deeds and acts of villainy.[6] For Carlos Monsiváis, the book goes far beyond a mere reproduction or appropriation of European literary trends as it recreates the atmosphere of the 1940s and embodies an emerging social class, all the while questioning the direction of the national project that created the class itself.[7] Cristopher Domínguez recognizes the historical value of the first Mexican urban novel he says occupies the claustrophobic space of an apartment.[8] Sara Sefchovich considers the work ahead of its time, yet probably not given its due because it didn't employ earth-shattering techniques like Fuentes' collage in *Where the Air Is Clear*.[9] Both Carlos Monsiváis and María Luisa Puga agree that the fate of this novel would have been different had it been handled by a more prestigious publisher.[10] But Vicens' publishing opportunities were limited by an exclusionary cultural policy that worked against women and sought out the most exotic narrative techniques. Aline Petterssen states: "If Juan Rulfo wrote two books where the specters of rural life wander about scorched by the wind and the sun, Josefina Vicens shows us the anguish of those immersed in the oppressive urban life that takes on the most inhuman anonymity."[11] Fabienne Bradú emphasizes the vast narrative complexities of the book, its connection with the author's own literary quest, and its ability to speak for an entire social class through the use of a first-person narrator. For Bradú, "in order to understand what happens in *The Empty Book*, one has to understand what happens during the act of writing, both the book's theme and the expression of its theme."[12] Sergio Fernández finds close connections between *The Empty Book* and novels written in 1928 by two of the "Contemporáneos," Xavier Villaurrutia's *Dama de corazones* and Gilberto Owen's *Novela como nube*.[13] María Luisa Puga feels that one of the most important aspects of the novel is that "it uses highly crafted writing to give the reader the ability to appropriate literary language because it lays bare both the writing process and the insecurities of those who are beginning a literary career." For Puga, *The Empty Book* is one of the most important Mexican novels of the modern period.[14] Elena Poniatowska feels that the wealth of sociological knowledge in both of Vicens' novels merits putting them alongside Samuel Ramos' and Octavio Paz's social essays.[15] For Josefina Vicens, this breadth of recognition was not easily achieved.

The Empty Book won the prestigious Xavier Villaurrutia Prize in 1958, yet the prophecy regarding the colorless fate of his own work that José García makes in his journal had come to pass. Prejudicial editorial policies, Vicens' disinterest in and disillusionment with the self-promotion game, and the understated nature of the book all converged to allow *The Empty Book* to slip into oblivion. Not until 1978, after the metafiction boom had peaked in Mexico, did Vicens' novel—which had clearly begun that phase of Mexican fiction—finally go into a second edition. Vicens included the Octavio Paz letter in this and all subsequent editions, perhaps attesting to her need, perceived or real, to have that powerful cultural figure support and/or legitimate her first novel. The letter appears in this translation because of its value as a cultural document. Most critics agree that had it not been for the publication of her second and last novel, *Los años falsos*, *The Empty Book* might well have been lost forever.

The confessional, the diary, and the autobiography are "literary" spaces that women have traditionally been allowed or encouraged to inhabit. In many ways, *The Empty Book* does not break with that tradition; rather, Vicens feeds upon it to find a place to speak from. By making José García try to create characters before our very eyes, Vicens questions the authority with which writers speak for others through the characters they have constructed. She puts her alter ego into situations that bring the ethics of writing into focus in order to examine the social responsibility of literature. By demystifying literature and using a highly accessible style that borders on the commonplace, Vicens opens the novel up to new readers. She further challenges readers by making them voyeurs, trespassers who violate José García's most private refuge, his journal. Even though Vicens consistently denied any premeditated theoretical intent behind her novel, all of the above, together with the erasure of the boundaries that comfortably separate fiction from reality, place us before a highly sophisticated, demanding work of literature written in deceivingly simple language. Far from being a mere intellectual exercise, *The Empty Book* reflects her own struggle with the written word. Since writing was problematical for her, Vicens used writing about writing to exorcise her own demons as she challenged the categories that sustained the canon.

The dedication—"To those who live in silence, I dedicate these pages, silently"—accentuates the work's marginal character and its very bold propositions calling attention to the silent aspect of the writing act and the contradictions it generates. But who are those living in silence? The most obvious answer might be that José García belongs to a whole emerging social class of mediocre, silent ones. However, since Josefina Vicens is José García, we can further read that in 1958, gay women writers, and perhaps all women, have no public voice. Like the author, they are forced to reproduce the most accepted forms of social representation. This explains the conventional appearance of José García's family, the role played by his nameless wife and by his illicit lover, Lupe Robles— "Lupe" being short for Guadalupe, the name of the Virgin, "Mother of Mexico." In the real world, it was Vicens' marriage to José Ferrel, a close friend of Salvador Novo, Xavier Villaurrutia, and Elías Nandino, that allowed her to leave home and establish an independent living situation. The two soon separated but continued to be friends until José Ferrel's death. Traces of anxiety mar *The Empty Book*, anxiety born of desire diluted by the need to comply with society.

Enhanced by the text's dialogue with itself and with its author, *The Empty Book* incarnates three interwoven searches: the author's personal quest, the literary quest, and the quest to find meaning in society. From the first page, Josefina and José García became indivisible. As several of her interviews and unpublished poems bear out, this was more than a literary strategy; it was the result of a natural inclination and the clear emergence of another part of herself after a long and painful struggle. Since José García is Josefina Vicens' double, we come to believe that, indeed, they are both striving to transcend their gray existence and achieve a measure of recognition by writing a novel of great import. This use of double identity also allows a woman to adopt a male voice and to act on a primarily male stage. Twenty years later, Clarice Lispector borrowed and modernized this same strategy in *The Hour of the Star* (1977). In addition to being a forerunner of the metafiction boom that would begin in the 1960s with novels like *Hopscotch* (1963), *Farabeuf* (1967), *Morirás lejos* (1967), *Obsesivos días circulares* (1969), and others, the search for literary form materializes in *The Empty Book* by questioning the ability of words to represent reality and, more important, by challenging the authority of writers who create powerful half-truths by using language to plunder worlds they know little or nothing about. Finally, the fact that the "real" narrative never begins means that José García and those like him never come to fruition; their search continues and they must remain before the void that their society has pushed them toward. Salvation won't be found by achieving some preconceived goal, but rather in understanding and embracing the process itself; the journey through the maze of words has somehow helped the character come to terms with himself as he is.

After struggling for several years with progressive blindness, deep depression, and other health problems, Josefina Vicens died in Mexico City and was buried in the SOGEM plot for writers on November 23, 1988, her seventy-seventh birthday. She left her house and other belongings on Pitágoras Avenue to the SOGEM, which plans to institute a Josefina Vicens Prize for excellence in writing.

—David Lauer

Notes

1. Daniel González Dueñas and Alejandro Toledo, *Josefina Vicens: La inminencia de la primera palabra*, essay no. 7 from the series Material de lectura (Mexico City: Universidad Nacional Autónoma de México, 1986), 5.

2. Adapted from ibid., 5.

3. Ibid., 6.

4. This anecdote was related to me by Casillas in a 1989 interview.

5. Dueñas and Toledo, 14.

6. Marta Robles, *La sombra fugitiva: Escritoras en la cultura nacional* (Mexico City: UNAM, 1986), 69–79.

7. Taken from a 1989 interview with Monsiváis.

8. Taken from a 1989 interview with Domínguez.

9. Taken from a 1989 interview with Sefchovich.

10. Taken from a 1989 interview with Puga.

11. Aline Petterssen, "Lo esencial en Josefina Vicens," *Hojas sueltas* (UNAM-Xochimilco) 3, no. 14 (July 1984): 10.

12. Fabienne Bradú, *Señas particulares: Escritora* (Mexico City: Fondo de Cultura Económica, 1987), 51.

13. Sergio Fernández, "Un retrato," *Hojas sueltas* (UNAM-Xochimilco) 3, no. 14 (July 1984): 8–9.

14. Taken from a 1989 interview.

15. Elena Poniatowska, "La miseria existencial del mexicano," *Excelsior*, March 29 and 31, 1982.

A Note on This Translation

THE EMPTY BOOK IS ABOUT THE WORLD OF CON-
tradictions; like reality, its language is deceptively simple. This
being so, I would like to mention some of the problems posed
by the original that I have interpreted to the best of my abili-
ties. José García is not a great writer. At times, his prose reflects someone who is trying to use words that he considers to
be writerly. He negotiates this with his own flat, highly constrained reality, the only thing he feels qualified to write about.
Vicens calls attention to the difference between a spoken and a
written discourse by making José García sound somewhat pe-
dantic at times; this is represented by his choice of words and
constructions, which he often comments on later in the text.
In still other instances García's prose is awkward, laden with
parenthetical expressions that interrupt his train of thought
and push his internal uncertainties into the foreground. These
interruptions often seem violent and effectively break the flow
of the narrative; they disrupt the comfortable progression of
linear thought.

Vicens' use of the passive voice is also very noticeable. Gen-
erally speaking, Spanish uses passive-voice constructions less
in common speech than English does. Vicens has used them
throughout the text to highlight García's alienation by placing
greater emphasis on the agent than on the actor. At other
times, José García uses the passive voice to depersonalize the
passage or to attempt to give it a higher level of abstraction.

To address these more abstract, philosophical questions, José García also mixes the impersonal *one*, which at times I translate to the more personal English *you*, with the more collective *we*. Vicens weaves these different levels of discourse to create movement between the individual, confessional voice, the abstract, anonymous voice, and the collective voice.

In many ways, *The Empty Book* can be considered an experimental novel. Vicens speaks to the conflict between reality and desire rather clearly throughout the book, but at times she erases the linguistic borders, which results in a subtle intermingling of different planes of reality. José García shifts in and out of a concrete present and a plausible future; his hypothetical utopia is constantly conditioned by the present. José García's imagination becomes so concrete that he uses the present tense to live out his fantasy, the future to deepen it, and the conditional to make it even more elaborate.

My version of *The Empty Book* is full of what today would be considered sexist language. Although Spanish allows a translator to choose between the masculine and feminine forms, I decided to make these generic third-person references masculine because of the period when this novel was produced and because Vicens herself uses the word *man* throughout the text. It is interesting to note that Vicens resemanticizes the concept of *man* to include women in the Grand Waltz episode. Although the book itself is a challenge to the gender system, I do not think Vicens would have approved of the kind of radical interpretation of her work that a completely nonsexist translation would have implied. The English language has yet to solve this problem in such a way as to make this possible for certain structures without rendering them impossibly awkward for the reader.

*A Letter
of Preface
by
Octavio Paz*

I RECEIVED YOUR BOOK. THANK YOU SO MUCH for sending it to me. I just finished reading it. It's wonderful, a true novel: simple, refined, and full of a secret pity but, at the same time, solid and forceful. It's admirable that with a theme like "nothingness," which has recently lent itself to so many philosophical essays both good and bad, you have been able to create from the "empty" intimacy of your character a complete world, our world, the world of the petty bourgeoisie. Naturalism? No, because your hero's reflections, always before the barrier of meaningless, crude events, go beyond all reproduction of apparent reality and show us man's consciousness and his limitations, his ultimate impossibilities. Man is always walking on the edge of the void, on the rim of the gaping mouth of insignificance (in the broad sense of the word). And, here, I would like to add a thought in passing: your book belongs to the literature of insignificant people—clerks, ordinary people—a philosophy that confronts the radical nonsignification of the world and the situation of modern man, who confronts a society that endlessly orbits around itself and has lost the sense and purpose of its actions. Aren't these the most noteworthy characteristics of the art and thought of our time? Isn't this what is called "the spirit of the time"?

Isn't recovering the meaning of history (personal or social, intimate or collective life), confronting death, ruin, chatter, and violence with creation one of the artist's missions? Far beyond any of the imperfections or weaknesses diligent critics might find in your novel, this is what you have achieved in *The Empty Book*. Well, then, what does your hero, that man who "has nothing to say," tell us? He tells us "nothing," and the mere fact that he actively assumes it makes that nothing, which is a part of all of us, become everything, an affirmation of the brotherhood and solidarity of all people. And so an "individualistic" book becomes fraternal, because every person who assumes his solitary condition and the truth of his own nothingness also takes on the inescapable condition of men of our age and can participate and share that general fate.

And now I want to confide something personal to you: Both the impossibility of writing and the need to write exist, knowing that you say nothing even though you may have said everything. There is also the awareness that only by saying *nothing* will we be able to conquer nothingness and affirm the meaning of life. I, too, in my own way, have felt this and attempted to express it in many texts, such as, for example, *¿Aguila o Sol?* and some poems in other books. I don't say this out of a vain desire for literary precision but for the simple pleasure of pointing out our like-mindedness. Now that discord and divisive rage reign in so many spirits, it's wonderful to discover that we concur with someone and that there really are affinities between people. I believe that those who know they have nothing have everything: shared solitude and brotherhood in the midst of defenselessness, struggle, and searching.

Thank you again for *The Empty Book*, so direct, so vital, and filled with so many things.

Octavio Paz
September 1958

The Empty Book

I NEVER WANTED TO DO IT. I'VE HELD OUT FOR twenty years. Twenty years hearing: "You have to do it . . . , you have to do it." Hearing it from myself. But not from that self who understands, suffers, and rejects it. No, from the other one, the underground one, from that self fermenting in me with a strange warmth. I say it sincerely. Believe me. It's true. Besides, I'll explain it in simple terms. This is the only way to be pardoned for it. But first, I want this well understood: I use the word *pardon* in the same way that a piece of fruit would use it when, inevitably, in spite of itself, it rots. The fruit would have to know that it is an unavoidable transformation. Anyway, it would, I think, be a little ashamed of its state: of having come, without original impurities, of course, to a sort of final impurity. This is something similar, very similar.

When I say, "to be pardoned for it," I mean pardoned for what I have finally become, but not for my life or for the process itself. There is something powerful and independent that acts inside me, watched over by me, contained but never conquered by me. It's like being two. Two who constantly run around chasing each other. But sometimes I've asked myself: who chases whom? All sense ends up being lost. The only thing that worries me is that they never catch up to each other. However, it must have already happened, because here I am, writing.

Ah, I wish I could explain how pathetic this union is! I don't know whether it's this half of me, the half I think I can still rely on, the one I speak to, which, exhausted, has subjugated itself to the other so that everything will be finished once and for all; or if it is the other one that I reject and berate, the one I have fought against for so long, who finally stands proud and victorious.

I don't know. At any rate it's a defeat, but perhaps a defeat that I sought or even desired. How will I ever know? I just know that a moment would be enough, this one, or that one, or this one . . . any moment. But many have already gone by; those I wasted, saying they could be the final ones, have already gone by. It would be enough not to write another word, not a single one . . . and I would win.

Well, not all of me; but yes, that half of me that I sense behind me right now, spying on me, hoping that I will write down the last word; watching how I go on dragging out the "explanation" of the way he might win, when I know perfectly well that explaining it is just what defeats me.

Not to write. That's all. Not to write. That's the formula. Stand up right now, wash my hands of it and flee. Why do I say "flee"? Simply go away. I have to be simple. I should go away; then I won't have to explain anything. I should put down a period and end here. That's all. A common, ordinary period that doesn't look as if it's the last one. Disguise the final period. Yes, that's right. Here.

That's it, but for whom? I want to clear this up. (It's only a small, momentary digression, then I'll go away.) I don't want to write. But I want to notice that I'm not writing, and I want others to notice it, too. I want to *quit* and not merely *abstain*. They both seem to be the same. Yes, I know they seem to be the same. It's discouraging! Nevertheless, I know they're not equal. On the contrary, I know they're absolutely different, terribly different. Because to quit means to have fallen and, at the same time, to have come out alive. It's the true victory. And, to abstain is too big a victory, without a fight, without any wounds.

There it is again! It always happens. After something is written, or even when I'm writing it, it begins to change by itself, gradually leaving me naked. Now I think that what is important and valuable is precisely to abstain. That struggle, those wounds I mentioned before so . . . pompously . . . are nothing more than the stage-set and scenery for my attitude.

Why begin a battle that I want to win if I know beforehand that I'll win by not beginning it?

It's a lot easier just not to write.

But then it turns out that the decision to abstain remains in the shadows, hidden forever. And that intention is what I'm interested in shedding light on. I need to say it. I'll begin by confessing that I've already written something. Perhaps, something like this, explaining the same idea. Forgive me. I have two notebooks. Somewhere in one of them it says:

TODAY, I COMPARED THE TWO NOTEBOOKS. That way I'll never be able to finish. I stubbornly insist on writing in this one everything that, later, provided I consider it of interest, I'll refine, finalize, and copy down in the second one. The truth is that notebook number two is empty, and this one's full of useless things. I thought it would be easier when I decided to use this system, that every three or four nights I'd be able to transfer to notebook number two selections from whatever I might have written in this one that I call number one, which is a sort of generous, tolerant well in which I'm tossing everything that I'm thinking about, without order or design. But the problem comes later when little by little I select, recover, and put down in notebook two what, corrected and polished, I really think will make up the book.

No. I don't think I'll ever do it.

It surprises me to be able to write: "I don't think I'll ever do it." But tonight, I'm calm, serene, and passively resigned to failure. It also surprises me to be able to write the word *passively*, applying it to myself, because I had reserved it for my mother. I was thinking: when I describe her in some part of the book, I'll use the term *passively* many times. I have to reveal this at that word's expense. For myself I had prepared others. Today, it doesn't matter if I use that one. Tonight I'm being truthful. (I don't like this last word: it's hard, ironlike, with a hook on the end. In notebook two, I'll get rid of it.) I'm being sincere. Tonight I'm sincere.

I know I won't be able to write. If I finish it, I know the book will be another one of millions that nobody talks about and nobody remembers. Sometimes I repeat my name: "José García." I see it written on each page. I hear people saying: "José García's book." Yes, I admit it. I often do this and I like it. But suddenly, everything comes crashing down.

Absurd! My God, how absurd! If the book doesn't have that miraculous, unspeakable thing that makes common words, words heard thousands of times, lash out and astonish; if each page can simply be turned without making the hand tremble a little bit; if the words can't stand up by themselves without the foundations of an argument; if simple emotion can't be found without searching for it, if it isn't present in every line; then what is a book? Who is José García? Who is that José García who wants to write, who needs to write, who every night sits down hopefully before a blank notebook and stands up exhausted and breathless after having written four or five pages that have none of this?

Today I'm resting. Today I speak the truth. I won't ever be able to write. Why, then, this overwhelming need? Because I know only too well that I'm nothing more than an ordinary man of limited talents with sufficient ambition in all the other areas of my life. A common man, nothing more. A man equal to millions and millions of other men. Oh, I wish someone would answer me! Why do I have this obsession? Why this maladjusted pain? Why can't my book have the same high standard as my need for writing it? Why does this splendid urgency inhabit such a dark, common place?

I thought it would be easy to start. I opened a notebook I'd bought for the express purpose. I prepared a plan, a sort of outline. With block print and carefully drawn Roman numerals, I wrote: "Chapter I.—My MOTHER." But I felt the fear immediately. No. I can't start with that. Since I have nothing important to say, it might seem that I begin, take my first steps, by babbling. All of you might think that I'm clinging to my mother's skirt so that I won't fall as I did as a child.

So, in order to write something, I had to lie to myself: I write for myself and not for others, and therefore I can recount whatever I please: my mother, my infancy, my park, my school. Is it that I can't remember them? I'm writing them for myself, to feel them close again, to possess them. A child, like a man, doesn't own more than what he invents. He uses what exists, but he doesn't own it. A child sees everything through his involuntary innocence, just as a grown man sees everything through his innate ignorance. The only way we can take deep possession of the beings and things and surroundings that we use is by returning to them through memories or by inventing them and giving them a name. What did I know of my mother when I was nine years old? Only that she existed. "Mom's sleeping . . . Mom's gone out . . . Mom's gonna get angry . . ." Then we were too real to be able to realize what we were, too present to realize what we were really like.

But I was, of course, deliberately lying. I don't write for myself. You say that, but deep down you've got a need to be read, to go beyond yourself; there is a desire for grandeur, for conquest. Then I thought I couldn't use personal feelings and situations that would diminish and localize the book's interest. The struggle to capture the concept, the whole idea, from the pile of chaff accumulated in notebook number one is the difficult part. From the preceding paragraph, for example, I like this: "by returning to them through memories, in order to possess with a greater consciousness that which we commonly only use." I'm thinking: "Around this, around this I've got to build something!" But the sentence is so dry now, so dead, lacking the warmth it had when I used it to justify myself.

I THOUGHT, ONCE, THAT THE TWO-NOTEBOOK system wasn't a good one. I could never find anything worthy, anything successful or interesting enough, to put down in number two. I decided that I had to be direct, and, with courage, I made myself write without stopping, determined to begin. The next day, I had to go back to the old method. All I had written was: "Here I am, trembling, poised, waiting for the ideas that don't come. It's a difficult moment. In the beginning, you don't know how to snare the reader with the first word, to snare the reader or to snare yourself. You can be your own reader, your only reader, that doesn't matter. I want it well understood: I write for myself.

"Full of eagerness, I listen to the house's noises; I direct my gaze everywhere. A suggestion, a memory, a voice . . . it has to . . . come from somewhere.

"Noises! What can I learn from them? I know them so well that they bore me. There's one: the tender murmuring of a woman who comes and goes as she putters around. By the number of her steps I know exactly where she is and where she is going. In the kitchen, the discreet, personal noise is accompanied by another peculiar and bothersome one. It seems simply that someone enters the kitchen, puts the plates, the silverware, and the spigot into motion. The clinking of dishes and the sound of dripping water get on my nerves. And then, inevitably, something falls. So much the better if it breaks, because then the noise ends abruptly and has a sort of dramatic justification. It's terrible, though, when those aluminum lids keep trembling on the floor in a ridiculous way, never suffering any damage from the fall. It's inevitable: when she enters the kitchen, I have to keep quiet, bracing myself so that the racket won't take me by surprise. This makes me lose some time, but, deep down, I should admit that it pleases me to find an excuse to go blank for a while, to authorize a moment's rest."

That was it. Naturally, I didn't use it. It's of no interest. I don't know how I started to write about those domestic noises that have been heard so much that nobody listens to them anymore. Perhaps it came out because of my fear of what happens next: she approaches and enters my room, drying her hands. Then, while they're still moist, she puts them on my head and asks, as she does every night: "Are you tired?"

Before hearing my answer, she glances at the almost empty

notebook. Why does she look at the notebook? Why does she ask me? How am I going to reply that, yes, I am worn out, exhausted because I haven't written a single line? How is she going to understand if, in the meantime, she has done a lot of hard work, walked all around the house, fetching, carrying, washing, cleaning . . . ? How is she going to understand that those things one can do while thinking about others don't wear you out like those that can't be done even when thinking about them constantly, profoundly, and even excruciatingly? What is real, what can be seen, nevertheless, is that she has worked and I haven't. She comes in and asks me if I am tired, and I don't know how to reply. Then, furiously, I put the notebook aside. Her tenderness irritates me and, even knowing that it doesn't exist, I pretend that I perceive a note of irony in her question and I answer violently, "Tired of what? You've already seen it. I haven't done anything. You, on the other hand, must be worn out! For the past two hours you've been doing important things!"

She stays quiet for a moment. Then she says, "Important, no, but they have to be done. . . . And yes, I am tired. Goodnight."

It's over! Now the shame of having been unfair! She's always right, so severe and efficient. Everything clean and transparent belongs to her. She is, and has been all her life, a beautiful lake unashamed of its murky depths. If you lean out over it, you see everything; you throw a rock into it and you can follow its journey and see the place where it finally comes to rest. Neither doubt nor anxiety remains, only remorse.

And then, looking for reconciliation, coming up with an excuse . . . . the best thing to do is to resort to common explanations: fatigue, nerves. Even though it's really something else. I would like to say to her: "I treat you badly because your composure bothers me, because I can't tolerate your simplicity.

I treat you badly because I detest people who aren't their own
enemies."

But . . . how am I going to say this to someone who is
supported by her own framework, who feeds on her righ-
teousness and the fulfillment of her duty, of her worthy and
silent servitude!

I can't tell her: "Forgive me, you're right. I'm treating you
badly because I've spent the entire night determined to do
something impossible, something beyond my capabilities . . .
because you found out, and that embarrassed me."

I can't, because it would bring on one of those sentimental
scenes that make her say things she doesn't believe, things that
make me feel as if my face were being smeared with sticky
ointments: "Don't take it that way. Don't give up . . . of course
you can write! Your problem is that you're tired. Tomorrow
it'll go better, you'll see."

Lies! Deep down she doesn't believe I can write a book, either; and she doesn't care if I write or not! In other words: she
doesn't care what I write. She would like it if I could, but only
because it would calm me down. She sees everything in terms
of my body: my weight, my stomach, my throat . . . . She
chooses not to step in directly, and the pent-up resentment
builds up because she can sense my discouragement.

One day, the only time, she was daring: "Forget that crazy
idea, you're killing yourself! I don't know why you are so bent
on writing!"

Right then, I could have killed her!

But she does it for my own good, or for what she thinks is
my own good. I understand it perfectly. That makes the situation more difficult because I can't avoid treating her harshly
every time she sees me writing and asks me about it, because
she thinks I find it flattering.

And later come the explanations, the excuses, and I have to

watch over myself so that I won't fall into needing to be consoled, into confessing to her what I don't want to confess to anyone. Then I become afraid to speak. I wish it were enough to move closer to her and look deep into her eyes. Words! Words that have to be explained, that have to be weighed and answered. And then to apologize! That's what I'm most afraid of, because then she asserts her ideas that are right at the same time that they're not. I understand this but I can't explain it.

My grandmother asked me to forgive her one day, a tender and arrogant apology I'll never forget. I was her favorite grandson and deserved the distinction because she was my favorite grandmother. It's true that I never met the other one who lived in Spain, who didn't interest me in the least, but I was sure to let her know: "My sisters say we have another grandmother . . . they might have another one, but for me you're the one and only."

I said it to flatter her, but one day, when we received a letter of mourning from Spain announcing my grandmother's death, I felt a strange sense of remorse. It made me remember that grandmother for a longer time than it took my sisters, who had never denied her existence, to forget her completely.

My grandmother said things that I liked when we were alone but embarrassed me in the presence of my sisters or the neighborhood children. She would always compare me to flowers. It seemed that the only beauty in the world could be found in flowers, but that lent an excessively feminine tone to her tenderness that I couldn't stand except when we were alone: "My little rose of Castile, my little rose of Jericho, my rose button!"

I didn't dare ask her not to say those things to me in public. Nevertheless, one day I started bombarding her with questions: "Grandma, what's Jericho?"

"Jericho, my child, is where the most beautiful roses grow."

Surely she didn't know where Jericho was, because she immediately added: "Those are some precious roses, that's what the books say. And you are my little rose of Jericho."

"But . . . Grandma. Please don't call me that . . . !"

It was impossible. She would laugh at those buds of manliness, hug me, and again call me her little rose of Castile, of Jericho, and of other places that I can no longer remember.

I CAN'T GO ON. I CAN ALREADY SENSE IN THE reader's spirit that tolerant contempt for those who have recounted things that are of concern only to themselves. I see written, written by me, those sentences that make me tremble when I remember them and nevertheless stand naked and sappy because they no longer have, and my writing can't make them have, what made them respectable and moving: my grandmother's trembling lips; her low tone of voice; her black dress, poor and dignified; her bony hands; her tired gestures. I know that when I say it like this, her traits seem to be a list of meaningless characteristics. If I could only give the whole and exact impression of what shined through that bearing of hers: her dignity, her special odor, her trembling; through those dresses that were always cut the same way; through all that made up her discreet and voluntarily hidden personality. If I could only reveal what she tried to keep hidden but what, because of its strength, came gushing out with great vigor. If I could do all that, any tale I might write about her would have the correct intensity and scope.

But I can't talk about her like that. It would be like dismantling her, like exhibiting her without the least modesty. I can't do it.

She asked me to forgive her one day, a sudden, tender apology that I'll never forget. That's all I can say.

And I think that's how this will go on, without my having anything to say, because the first thing I wrote down in big letters, like an arrow shouting out a warning, was: "Do Not Speak in First Person." That inevitably leads to the telling of personal things that are limited to the exact dimensions of the family home, to near relatives, the neighborhood, the neighbor. I want to write something that will interest everybody. How can I say it? . . . by using not the inner voice but the great murmur.

It's so hard! I need a narrow path. I need to restrain myself, constantly restrain myself.

If I were to title the first chapter, which I still haven't written, "My Mother," it would reflect the idea that, by describing her accurately, I would clear up many things about myself, things about my adulthood that I'm interested in emphasizing. Precisely because I was running away from myself, I wanted her to be a key, an initial sign.

I need to explain it. It wasn't that I wanted to tell my life story chronologically, from its roots to its fruits, attached to my mother's skirt in the beginning and pulling my children along by the hand in the end. No. My God! What can a man like me say about his life? Nothing has ever happened to him before now, and he can't tell what's happening to him now because that's precisely what is happening to him: he needs to recount it and isn't able to. But it has nothing to do with events, with happenings, with dates, characters, or endings.

No. How can I say it? It has to do with writing and, therefore, one has to single out a theme, but more than singling it out, since I don't have one that will interest everybody, I have to make it disappear, dissolve into the words themselves. Words again! How they torment me. The truth is that I can't invent anything or anybody and, therefore, need to fill that hole, that initial void, with words, but with such words, such convincing words, that the presence of the hole won't be noticed. I don't want it to be a mere putting-down, filling-out, or insertion of words, but rather a transformation of words until the void disappears, without a theme, without matter.

It's true that this idea was the result of my lack of imagination. My goal in the beginning was to write a novel, to create characters, to give them names and ages, ancestors, professions, and interests; to interconnect them, weave them, make them depend on each other, and make of each one a vigorous and attractive or perhaps a repugnant or fearsome example.

It was horrible! I remember it like a nightmare. I was obsessed. I would write down sentences that all of a sudden came to mind and would, I thought, do very well or be suitable for the moment when "Elena set off on the journey." I would observe people's faces in the street, on buses, in movie theaters, in order to later put together, with that mouth and this nose, the faces of my characters. If I were lucky enough to find a noteworthy physical trait, I felt happy and, of course, began to compose the passage with great enthusiasm: " . . . it was an insolent nose that refused to blend in with the rest of the face. The eyes, the beard, the mouth, the cheekbones always seemed to be chasing after it. That pursuit made them age: the nose was the only young thing about the face . . . ."

And that seemed to be original to me, that overelaborated, incredibly absurd passage!

I satisfied my desire to have some of my characters turn out to be pleasant by limiting them constantly to saying friendly things until I realized that by robbing them of the complex totality of man I was depriving them of life. I fell into the terrible habit of emphasizing, exaggerating, believing that in this way I gave strength to the trait. Naturally, the result was that the characters turned out to be false. It also happened that after outlining—completely, in my opinion—the personality of my character, I didn't know what to do with him. I could have made him move had I only conceded that he resembled my Uncle Agustín, for example, whom I knew intimately and who was a quite attractive and interesting subject. But my pretense to create, not to recreate or take advantage of already existing types, kept me from falling back on that concession which I considered dishonest. It wasn't a question of experience and knowledge but of imagination, an imagination which I completely lack because, despite all my efforts, I couldn't invent even a halfway interesting plot. Nor could I even manage to create a decent setting. I realized that it was essential to create the right habitat and to furnish it properly so that my characters might move about with ease, giving each one his own position and surroundings. Yes, it was essential. But I know nothing of styles or epochs. I've always had a house with very modest comforts, one that's acceptable and, like most homes, keeps filling up with objects as the family grows. Sometimes, as an exception, somebody buys something frivolous but almost always we buy only what is absolutely necessary. That's why something always stood in my way when I tried to create different surroundings. I understood that in the regal house of "Don Augusto de la Rosa"—a character that I'd invented with great effort—there had to be porcelain and marble. But I couldn't say, concisely, revealing little refinement: "there was porcelain and marble." No. One can say about a poor house, "there were three chairs and an old sofa," and it works just fine because an impoverished description deepens the drama of the misery that one intends to accentuate. The lack of adjectives gives a more appropriate impression of the poverty of the surroundings. But it seemed to me that opulence could only be described with opulent language, and that the porcelain and marble merited at least some reference to their antiquity and origin.

So, it became illegal for me to work exclusively with characters of my own social class and limited resources in order to make the narrative more accurate and easier for me. It was the well-trodden, hackneyed road. And to make myself consult specialists' books in order to copy dates, collect information about dynasties and industrial regions, and gather other facts seemed crafty and dishonest. So it was that I never managed to create anything real with any of the settings: the rich people's houses turned out to be dismantled, empty, and ridiculously adorned with "luxurious" furniture and "fine" tapestries, adjectives that only revealed my absolute ignorance. And the middle-class houses turned out to be equally unreal for me because of the great care that I took not to fall into the trap of describing an exact copy of my own house. I distorted my desire for originality, imagining what might have come out well had I only observed and, later, simply conveyed it.

Because of all of that, of course I couldn't create live characters, or interesting plots, or adequate settings. Now I can say it this way, with ease, free from the worry of depicting them. But, for a long time, during endless nights of continuous effort, nights filled with anguish, I insisted on putting absurd characters into absurd situations in which they didn't feel, speak, or move like human beings. If they ever got sick, they were always deathly sick. If they cried, the way men sometimes cry, it wasn't simply because they were alive, but because something terrible and ghastly had happened to them. They never showed a faint smile caused by some far-off and agreeable event but always had a superficial smile to react to what another character had said three lines earlier. They never spoke of just anything. They didn't spit, either. They never did anything ordinary, spontaneous, or instinctive.

And it's not that I'm thinking at this moment that obviousness is most appropriate for mirroring reality. It's not that I'm claiming that, in order to be real, a character has to spit in public. No. It's that I understand that he should be sketched with features so natural and relaxed that he could spit at any moment, even when he might not do it during the entire story.

I didn't get anywhere. That's the truth. Now, I don't strive to imagine, I don't strive to invent. All that's left is this tormented need to write something, and I don't know what it is.

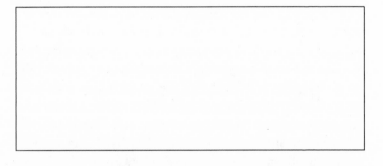

I COME INTO THIS LITTLE ROOM WHERE I WRITE, take the pen and the notebooks, and look everywhere apprehensively, as if I were a novice, an inexperienced thief.

I've got some of that deep inside me. I'm part novice. Only in part because I split myself there, too. I rob myself. Like a thief, I steal another drop from my own dry conviction not to write, those last drops that are left when a person dries up from the outside in and not the other way around. I don't know if I'm explaining myself. I mean: when you don't dry up all by yourself but because of yourself. To dry up by yourself is to lack that element that moistens and conserves freshness. And to dry up because of yourself is to make that element willingly disappear, to drain it from yourself in order to cause dryness. In the first case, the last drop is never left. In the other, it's there, betraying one's intent, always hidden and ready to flower, easily exposed to thieves.

And that's my situation. One "self" has dried up because of himself, not by himself, and the other one, who knows it, also knows that he will always find some way to steal those last drops. When that happens, the two of them begin to write.

I wish I could name them, give each one a name just as I've given each notebook a number. Oh, if I only knew which one to trust and which one to defend myself from. Because, sometimes, the "self" who does what I don't want to do is, in reality, the one whom I love because he releases me from that stubborn, hermetic *no* that I am bound to.

Sometimes, the one I admire is the other one who tries to tighten his knots and lock his doors. But it so happens that even though these two seek different ends, they always meet in the same place: in a notebook where one writes in order to explain, in order to show why he shouldn't write, and the other one writes in order to deny his right to demonstrate this, even if his own demonstration needs to be written.

It's very clear: there are just two sentences. One: I have to write because I need to, even when it's only to admit that I don't know how. And the other: since I don't know how, I just shouldn't write.

Nevertheless, both are written: one by the clumsy but also loyal and modest hand that I haven't ever been able to hold back, and the other by that conscious, cold hand that always takes up the pen, sure that it's for the last time, and will only pick it up again in order to counteract the impulse of its enemy.

I'd like to give those two "selves" a name, to get to know them a little better, to deal with them. This is, apparently, meaningless, since they are both me. But, in reality, somehow they're no longer part of me. Neither one nor the other. It seems that both ruthlessly plunge headlong into their own thoughts, and I feel as though each time they leave me farther behind.

There are times when the clash becomes so apparent, so violent, that I have to step in in order to calm them down. Naturally, I'd like to agree with the one who thinks I shouldn't write. And I would agree with him if I could say it the only way it can be said: with silence. But since he wants to be heard, he uses the other's method, only without his humility. Then I approach the other one, who moves me because I understand that at least he uses his voice to say things he doesn't know how to express, instead of saying that he doesn't say it because he doesn't know how. The first one has an honest and lively expression, a kind of sincerity. The second one, who would be right only if he were to say nothing, is serious and aware as well as cowardly. The terrible thing is that both know how wrong it is to write nothing more than this, this something that is nothing that either of them can do anything about.

A LITTLE WHILE AGO MY SON, JOSÉ, CAME INTO the room, as he often comes to see me when I'm writing. He asks me questions and shows interest: "Are you very far along in your book, Dad?"

Far along! I keep thinking: "How can I move ahead in a book that is stiff and constrained in order to hide this double impotency: my inability to write and my even greater inability to keep from writing?"

Of course, my son believes that each new line is a step forward. I can't tell him that each new word is a crushing retreat back to the first one, which is just as flimsy and insignificant as the last. Nor can I tell him that not one word's meaning is important enough to justify it, and that all the words together, those I've already written as well as those I haven't, will only form the awkward contour of a hole, of an essential void.

"It's a novel. Right, Daddy?"

And then, with that fascination for the silver screen typical for his age: "Does it have a happy ending?"

Violently, I just now told him to leave. He opened his huge eyes in surprise. I don't think I've done him any harm. I'm sure—how shameful to write it down—that his young, generous imagination will conclude: "Writers are so strange and different from other people!" And I hope that, in his eyes, I will appear to be not unjust but creative, one who has to be put up with because he's a writer.

Maybe he'll tell his friends, with a slight tone of pride in his voice: "My father writes. He's already well along in his book!" And perhaps one of his friends, a clerk's or businessman's son, will feel a certain envy at heart and wish that his father could also be a writer.

What a sham! I should have responded honestly to his sign of interest by saying: "I'm not a writer! I'm not! What you see here, this notebook full of words and erasures, is nothing more than the barren result of a desperate tyranny of some unknown origin. All of this and everything I'll be writing here is just to say nothing, and the end result will be a heap of full pages and an empty book. It's not a novel, son, and it doesn't have a happy ending. It can't finish what it doesn't begin because I have nothing to say. Your father isn't a writer, and he never will be.

He's a loser who needs to write the way others need to drink. It's just that that fellow does it and quenches his thirst. He doesn't give anyone an account of the path that private act takes: it's born, it's carried out, and it dies within him. It's called intoxication, and it's enjoyed or suffered alone. But writing is another thing. To write is to want to tell others, because all it takes to talk to yourself is an intense thought or a distracted murmuring between the lips. And you can't tell anybody anything when you don't have anything new to offer. But if a person's consciousness is keen enough to understand this, he shouldn't be weak in the face of the urge to speak out, and this urge should be so moderate that he'll be able to overcome it."

And that's the origin of this contradiction. Since I can't overcome it, I close my eyes like a coward and allow that error, that lie, to live on in my children, my wife, and, sometimes, myself. And it annoys me when they don't treat me with the tolerance that everybody else grants to those people from whom they expect something important and different. I, who know everything, have surprised myself by concealing my violent attitudes and arbitrariness, which I try to explain to myself as characteristic of those who have a loftier mission than the common people, who are both under their family's care and at its service. I know it's an ugly sham. My wife with her terrifying intuition also knows and, nevertheless, says nothing. But my children! José deceived and Lorenzo, the poor thing, still so little, suppressed all the time by his mother: "Good God, boy, be quiet, your father is writing!"

"Don't bother your father, boy, he's writing!"

This "cooperation," this "respect," makes me so ashamed that I lash out at her, at him, at the house, at everything.

"You make more noise hushing him up. Leave him alone!"

I say to the child: "Get to bed. Nobody can stand you!"

And the one that nobody really can stand is me.

The truth is that I can't expect more than the normal consideration that any wife shows for any husband. Doubtless, I could have improved my economic situation and worried about earning a little more money. My wife is tired, every day José needs more things—he's already in the second year of law school—and Lorenzo had always been so frail that doctor bills and medication are a permanent part of our budget. This boy disturbs me. He has a strange gaze, a vacant stare, a melancholy that isn't fitting for his age. His birth was so unexpected and, truthfully, so unwanted. I haven't forgiven myself for it. I'm sure that our cowardly rejection has affected him.

It's also true that I experience strange feelings that I'm ashamed to talk about. This is one of them, the most frequent one: even though for so many years I've been the same person and have done the same things, I don't know why I feel alien to myself. It's as if I had accidentally fallen into my body and, suddenly, come to recognize the place where I live.

My wife asks me why I keep looking at my hands when I wake up in the morning. Of course, I can't answer her. How do I know what I do on the subtle edge of waking! But, sometimes, I do it when I'm wide awake in the office, and I still can't explain it. It's something like an attempt to identify myself, a quick test of the truth of my physical existence. It's as if there were a serious breakdown between what I am and what represents me, as if, suddenly, I need to take note of myself.

I don't like my body. It's weak, flabby, and insignificant. No. I don't like it. Perhaps, for that reason, it has never mattered to me, and, so, I never take care of it. The result is that my body has imposed on me, in several installments, large or small annoyances: toothaches, colds, heart flutters, and a whole bunch of ailments. But, more than anything, a permanent inner trembling, a falling apart. It's like the certainty that something is going to happen, the fear that it may happen, and the impatience of waiting for it to happen. Sometimes, I wonder if that anguish isn't possibly the great anguish caused by the fear of death, which is only somewhat lessened by the habit of feeling it. It's not as if it's excessive, because I don't have to spend energy to weaken it. No. I feel it's my same size. What's so hopeless about it is not its dimensions but its permanence, its permanent residence inside me.

The other anguish, not being able to stop writing, has alternatives. At times, I feel that I don't suffer from it. I know that there are small, temporary separations that make me experience that pure sadness of being far from something that belongs to me, something to which I will not return but, nevertheless, from which I can distance myself for a time. But that anguish! That persistent, inexplicable anguish, bound to man like his own death!

There are times when I get drunk to numb it. And, yes, while drunk, I feel a sort of outer courage; a daring that exalts me and makes me happy. I leave myself, leave my trembling, leave my death behind. Where do I go? Perhaps to the very place from which I was trying to escape. A person can't completely reinvent himself, but at least I feel armed. When I come back, I wouldn't know how to describe those arms. I couldn't even do it when I'm out there because they aren't added to me or placed on me, but they make up a part of me. I don't know what they're like. I just know that they meet my needs. If someone were to ask me: "What are you feeling?" I would only be able to say: "I feel like it doesn't matter!" But if he insisted on knowing what doesn't matter to me, I wouldn't be able to answer. It's a very thin idea. It still interests me but without mattering to me. There's a great difference, I'm sure of it. Perhaps I could explain it, but I know that then the idea would grow, would widen, and then wouldn't pass through where it passes when I'm out there.

But how I would love to be able to return with the idea and explain it without doing it the least bit of damage! It's a little like this: being drunk doesn't relieve me of my suffering, but it gives the suffering another meaning . . . like a pain that's naturally a part of me, inside me, whose persistence doesn't make me suffer, because I don't perceive it. In other words, I find it natural for it to exist, as natural as my own existence.

Here, I've never been able to get used to the idea of existing. I'm always questioning, always restless, surprised at my own existence. There, it's not like that: to be is being itself. It's not like over here, a phenomenon surrounded by questions. It's a transparent event without the barrier of "why?", an event understood in itself. Out there I never tremble. I'm not afraid of dying because death has the same natural, integrated feeling that everything else has. It's just another simple fact, not a question.

As I get drunker and drunker, I start acquiring something I imagine to be true peace: not to get upset because one simply is, nor to become afraid because one can cease to be. There's a sort of internal accommodation and adjustment, and all of those things that stand out like jagged edges here are, perhaps, inherited, accepted belongings there that peacefully make a person whole.

What's more, the atmosphere is different. It's very difficult to give some idea of a setting that's not constructed with familiar elements, but, on the contrary, with unusual ones. The ease of movement is a good example. There are houses where it's hard to move around because they're inhibiting. There are others where movement is made easy from the start. Sometimes being drunk is like the feeling of going into a house where you can do or stop doing anything you want to. There's even an auditory sensation, believe me! I've heard it many times: the sound a chain makes when it falls. It's then, at that moment, that a man stands up straight and begins to move in a different way. The steps that usually lead to his house, to his job, to some specific place, now lead to another—without the sensation of guilt that sometimes goes along with choosing pleasure, without feeling that he's turning his back on something. No, he simply walks in the direction of desire. If something necessary was left behind, it doesn't matter because it's not considered necessary. The reason it's back there isn't because we've put it off, but simply because it's back there.

For me, being drunk isn't exactly losing my sense of things, it's changing my sense of things. But I want to be clear, I am not the one who changes it. That would be the same as a substitution, something temporary. Things have another meaning in and by themselves and, since I'm not aware of the mechanics of change, I suddenly find myself facing them and feel that they're permanent, exact, and appropriate. I feel good—not because I might remember that I was feeling bad before and now notice the change. No, I simply feel good.

I know it, because the awareness of that sensation begins when I'm not aware of it anymore: when I'm here trembling again with my head hung low, listening to my wife's scolding and the discreet advice of my friends.

Because, you know what? Alcohol is really bad for me.

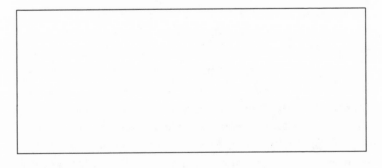

I'VE WON A SMALL VICTORY. TODAY MAKES EX-actly eight days that I haven't written. This relapse is just to record it. Eight days. I remember that last Wednesday I was on the verge of writing and was able to overcome the urge. Naturally, I used a trick. When I was about to enter my office . . . that expression is so presumptuous! Because also in the office are the sewing machine, a wardrobe, and some boxes where my wife keeps the most unlikely things that seem as if they'll never be of any use and, nevertheless, always are. Poor men's wives are a little magical. I remember that José wanted a tux when he turned eighteen. I didn't have any money but we bought it because my wife sold several things that she had kept in those very boxes, things I thought would never interest anybody. Who bought them from her? I never found out and have been too ashamed to ask her. The truth is that she always takes care of all the practical things. I'm totally useless. I work and I love her. And I love my children. That's all I do in life. I know that many people prosper, ambitious and capable people; but I really don't know how they do it. I don't have the faintest idea about business. It's completely beyond me. Business, even the most legitimate, makes me feel ashamed. I know this is stupid, really stupid, but it's true; it makes me ashamed. I used to buy things; it always turned out badly. "They rooked you," my wife would say. Now I prefer not to buy anything. When we go to the store or the market together, I always wait outside. I'm sorry, I can't stand it. The seller makes me suffer as much as the buyer. It seems to me that the seller makes an effort to pander his goods, that he has to overcome his modesty and his good taste because he needs to earn a few more pennies. The buyer also has to make an effort to hide his poverty; he shrewdly adopts an arrogant attitude so that the bargaining seems like malice instead of a reflection of his own misery.

But I'm talking about something else. I was saying that for eight days I was able not to write and that that evening, when I was about to do it, I restrained myself and spontaneously invited my wife to the movies. She was thrilled, since we are almost never able to go out. She was so happy that she aroused a kind of bold generosity in me. After paying for the tickets, I didn't have more than eight pesos left, but in my wallet I was carrying more than ninety-five that some office mates had given me to buy lottery tickets. "I'll pay them back somehow," I thought. "Let's see, how can I manage?"

As we left the theater, I made up my mind and struck a mysterious pose. I felt important. I took her by the arm and said: "We're going out on the town!"

We got into a cab and, while she was waiting for me to give the cabdriver our address, I said in a very natural, everyday tone: "The Great Waltz, please."

"What kind of a place is that, José? Heavens, you're crazy! Look at the rags I've got on!"

I stared at her and squeezed her hand. She was right to talk of rags. My hasty, even slightly impatient invitation hadn't given her time to change her dress or to put on one of the two or three that she has for going out. The coat that covered her housedress, which she didn't take off during the whole show in spite of the heat, was quite old.

We arrived at the Great Waltz and chose a quiet table. The classic types were at the others: they shout, pound the table, drink, swear that they are real tough, and give exaggerated tips because money doesn't matter; because they say women are inferior; because at work they can't shout; because alcohol is compassionate; and because they suffer, because they suffer. And it's all so that they can think they aren't suffering.

At the Great Waltz, some gloomy musicians play waltzes and so I had them play a few. I wanted my wife to listen to them and dream. I wanted her to forget about Lorenzo's constant illness and the fact that, starting a few weeks ago, José has been coming home late and pounding on the door. I know he has a woman, but my wife doesn't. His woman is a waitress, the one in the café at the corner by the house. Her name is Margarita, and my son is crazy about her. And I also know that any night now, perhaps tomorrow, he'll come into my room with his head hanging low, blushing in embarrassment, and he'll tell me what all sons tell their fathers at some point: "Dad . . . I want to talk to you . . . man to man!"

Man to man! What does my son think a man is? I think he thinks that a man becomes a man precisely when he has a woman.

José, José my son, if you only knew what a man is!

A man is . . . but do I even know? The only thing I can tell you is that you are a man, my loving, adolescent José. And I, José García, your father, in spite of my age, am still so insecure, astonished, and questioning. A man is that waiter who detests us and slightly ridicules my anxiety as I pay the bill and my fear that I may not have enough money. A man is that gray-haired musician in the threadbare suit who eagerly looks at the small bill I send him so that he will play, as mechanically as he does every night, a waltz that almost nobody hears. A man is also your mother, someone who does hear it, but now hears it through a dream watered down by the sad, repetitive years of sickness, work, debt, and worn-out, creaking furniture. Your mother who, in spite of all that, has right now in her eyes a delicate shine and a hint of surprise. A man is that fellow over there at the table: alone, disheveled, overburdened, he drinks fast and asks himself if "that woman" will ever show up. I could stay here long enough to follow the course of his drunkenness and to see the two men who live inside him. But I already know all about it: he was wandering around the streets because he didn't want to go to her house. You know what? A man always has a tiny reservoir that comforts him: his dignity. He says "that woman" with disdain, but "that woman" means "that one" in particular and none other. There's the mystery! The deepest mystery. Thousands of women walk the streets, women everywhere, but "that one" is the one he loves: "that woman" with her mouth and her eyes and her words, "that woman" alone. And he can't go to her house because he knows that, for her, he's not "that man." So he walks around and feels an oppressive pain, a pain whose weight he can't bear alone. But he can with six or seven drinks. So he goes to a place where, maybe, "that woman" will appear. She won't, but he'll wait for a long time until the alcohol, such a good companion, so tender and so warm, numbs his dignity and gives him the strength to go and knock on a door, precisely that one door that he never wanted to knock on to begin with. Tomorrow, he'll feel awful. But today, as well as tomorrow, he will have been just that: a man.

The only ones who perhaps aren't men are those who don't seem to be like the others, those who surpass or never measure up to them, those who grow or shrink until they are outside the normal bounds. They aren't men because they lack the polite standard of similarity.

Similarity is what makes love possible!

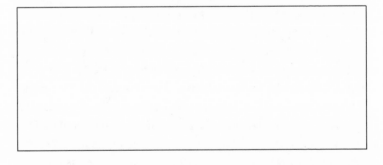

I'VE WRITTEN A LOT TONIGHT! AND ALL TO SAY that that Wednesday I was able not to do it. And what did I do today? I haphazardly told how I took my wife to hear music and how my son already has a lover. My God, just to say that?

How do writers do it? How do they get words to obey them? Mine go wherever they want, wherever they can. When I see them already written, when, shyly, I reread them gluttonously, they make me feel ashamed. I feel as though they keep breaking away from me and falling into my notebook, just falling formlessly, without premeditated placement.

I wish it were somehow different. For example, when I see a beautiful afternoon, I'd like to think: "I see that this afternoon is beautiful. The afternoon pleases me. It pleases me to feel what this afternoon makes me feel." I'd like to describe the afternoon and what I'm feeling. So what do I have to do? First, I think, to sense the afternoon. Then, to attempt to isolate its elements: light, temperature, and color. Then to observe its sky, the trees, the shadows: in short, everything that belongs to it. And when these elements are finally reflected in words, and that pleasurable quivering, that shuddering surprise that I feel as I contemplate it, is expressed, then, surely whoever might read my words, even myself, could find in my notebook a lovely afternoon and a man who senses and enjoys it.

And what if I were to try it that way, with that kind of system?

Well, I'd have to contemplate those afternoons or imagine or remember a little bit, because it's been so long since I've seen one. I leave the office at nine o'clock in the evening so worn out that I no longer have the eager sensibility I need for feeling what is around me. The only part of the afternoon that I can contemplate is the light that comes in through the little window in front of my desk, a light that seems to come out of nowhere, since I don't see the sky. Slowly, it gets dimmer and dimmer, dimmer and dimmer, until we turn on the fluorescent lamps that overpower it.

I don't know how many employees feel the way I do when those lamps go on. It's logical that it should happen that way, otherwise we couldn't work, but I can't believe they don't suffer the moment it happens or that they have become accustomed to having necessity—just like that without any runaround—rob them of enjoyment or, worse, substitute something artificial for what is natural, startlingly natural.

None of us remembers anymore how a day dies. Or how it is born, or how, at five o'clock in the morning, it seems unable to dawn, at noon unable to die, and at six in the afternoon, in its death throes, impossible to save.

I don't know about other men, but for those of us who have been working there, overcome and discouraged after so many years, a day has its magical hours that mold our feelings. We arrive in the morning happy and clean. We crack a few jokes and start to work. There's a kind of useful, lively rhythm, an effort we dedicate to someone, to our wives or our children, that makes us feel satisfied and even important. At two in the afternoon, burdened by the heat and confinement, we all reveal a wretched expression of fatigue, mostly physical, that diminishes the meaning and justification of the effort. There's a kind of hate for the body, for having to feed and dress it. There's a violent desire—I'll say it with the exact, crude word—for it to kick off once and for all. Obligation and poverty wrap themselves around our neck like a thick rope. We exchange hostile words and glances until our comrade, who is as tired and unfortunate as the rest of us, is no longer a comrade but an enemy. We detest him for the same reason that he detests us: because he's our equal, because he's similar, because it's inevitable: in other words, for the same reason that we loved him in the morning.

And at eight in the evening, without protests, already calmer and softened by weariness and the idea that we will soon leave, we all wear the same expression of having done our time for the day. And we all have that anxious need to seek shelter in those houses where our wives and children wait for us, those for whom we have done, and would do for the rest of our lives if we had to, that plain, anonymous, gray task that allows us to live together with our warmth, together with our love.

Oh, that cherished circle of starting the day for them and ending it with them!

ONE DAY, I REMEMBER IT VERY WELL, I WAS tempted to write in big letters: "Sometimes I regret having gotten married." I'm glad I didn't because it's a lie. I don't regret it. What happens is that sometimes, when I'm alone, when my family is already asleep and I know they are all resting securely and peacefully, I go back in time and back into myself and find myself next to the person I used to be before I had them. So many unfulfilled desires survive weakly inside me and suddenly appear, even though they are deadened by a long, thick distance.

For example, I remember when I decided to become a sailor. Back then I thought, "Nothing in the world will make me change my mind." I was fourteen. We were living on the coast. One evening while we were eating dinner, I announced my decision. I can still see my mother's eyes. They conveyed such grief in the very brief time that passed between my words and her gaze that she gave me the impression that she had foreseen my destiny and pictured her dead son. But she didn't say a word. My father, on the other hand, delivered a dramatic speech in which I could only understand that I was the sole male child, the hope of his old age, and the guardian of my sisters. I remember, as my father kept speaking, that what he was saying and the way he was saying it made me feel as if I were gradually being suffocated. It was the first time I felt the horror of being imprisoned, condemned without a prayer.

That same evening when everybody had gone to bed, I went out. The beach was dark and lonely. I lay down in the sand. I wept unconsolably for what was dying in me and even before it had a chance to live. I thought I was crying for myself, without really knowing that I was crying for man's two most bitter pains: love and the parting of the ways.

I DON'T LIKE TO REMIND MYSELF OF THAT. I don't like to bring up that long-gone adolescent who couldn't imagine that many years later he'd be talking about himself in this muted, stifled tone. Being able to write only from the point of view of my current age drives me insane. Some things can be written only with a smooth hand, and mine—I'm looking at it right now—is already wrinkled and bearing the spots of my years. I'm afraid to betray the young man I once was. I remember him so well! I feel him, clean and energetic, trembling inside me. But I know that's the very reason why I can't do it, because when I try to speak about him in this long-overdue notebook written with an old man's hand, my years, my weariness, and my pettiness will appear, and that splendid young man will come out covered and tainted by my ashes.

And since I couldn't let him breathe, since I smothered him inside of me, since I covered him a little bit at a time with the limelike earth of my life, since I could only provide a lukewarm place for him instead of the many passionate ones he wanted, I don't want to speak of him. I can't.

But I also think that if I don't speak about him who represents the best part of me, what am I going to talk about? About this man I am now? About what I have become? About this dark, plain man sunk deep into an anguish that he cannot clarify or justify because the reasons for it are unexplainable?

I guess it comes from the realization that on many occasions I feel deeply alone. The cherished, everyday company of my wife and my children isn't enough. Why can't I also have the company of any other man, of the human being who casually passes by me at that precise moment when I feel a warm, overwhelming desire for communication? Why can't it be that way? Why can't you offer to absolutely anyone, at a unique moment, the freshness of a word, an embrace, or a question?

No. We keep everything to ourselves and share it, if at all, with a very limited number of human beings, as if the rest of them didn't exist or were incapable of understanding or loving us.

I walk down any old street. Other men go by. I don't look at them nor they at me. We are equals and strangers so far away from each other it's as if we weren't even traveling along the same street. Perhaps we even share the same thought or stride. We are the same, and I'll never know anything about them, not even their names. That's when I feel strangely alone. I think the others feel the same, and an almost irresistible urge strikes me to approach someone naturally and use my tender human warmth—what would be better to use?—and ask him to chat for a while.

What stops me from doing it? What shyness or hardness holds me back? What coldness paralyzes my hands that are so willing to reach out and shake any other's without discrimination, premeditation, or prior knowledge of him? But I don't do it. I've never been able to. And the impulse stays inside me, quietly and silently, not daring to live, which is like dying before its time.

I walk on a little further and let everything pass by. I hardly even look out of the corner of my eye at what's around me. And I come to my house feeling a great emptiness that could have been filled just by uttering one word or stretching out my arms.

It's not a form of pity or commiseration toward others. On the contrary, I want it understood that it's an eagerness, an uncontainable yearning for mankind, for voices, for lives.

So I sink into myself. But to myself, I am like a tiny place I've visited before, looked over, gotten to know, and walked through until I could walk no more. Nevertheless, there is where I always end up and stop to talk to myself.

"You should've asked that guy who seemed so down on his luck something, anything. Maybe he was all alone. Maybe, like you, he had the need to talk. You should've done it. You should do it everyday. Think about it. It would be like taking a trip. You never travel either, José García. In a few years, you won't be able to say: 'That reminds me of what I saw once in such and such a place.' But you will be able to remember: ' . . . on such and such a day that fellow told me . . .'"

WHAT A LESSON THAT WAS! MY GOD, WHAT A lesson! Just one word was enough for him. Yesterday at noon, I left the office. I was preparing for it all morning long. And I did it. I went along walking slowly, not in the street because everyone was in such a hurry. Then I thought perhaps the right place would be a park with benches and trees. I went to Alameda Park* and strolled through as I observed attentively. Finally I decided.

On a bench there was a poorly dressed man with a stern expression on his face. He had his legs stretched out and his hands in his pants' pockets. He was staring off into the distance absentmindedly as if he were thinking about something. Not about different things. No. When thoughts wander from one place to another, one's expression changes. Sometimes they come upon a pleasant memory or desire and then the facial muscles soften imperceptibly. Or, suddenly, they harden, if one's thoughts have stumbled on something painful.

But if the expression stays the same, if the lips don't open slightly or close to block the exit of a word, if the eyes keep staring as if dead, and if the eyelids fall in time to the same unchanging rhythm, it's because one's thoughts are immobile.

That man was thinking about something. It was just one thing that, evidently, wasn't very pleasant. I sat down next to him and looked at him several times. He didn't notice my presence or the contrived movements I was making to attract his attention. So I offered him a cigarette. He looked at me, took it, and with a gloomy voice simply said: "Thanks." I lighted it for him with great care. "Thanks."

"I don't know if you like this brand. They're quite strong."

"Yes, thank you."

What else could I say to him? But I was determined. I had

---

*The Alameda is a spacious park in the center of Mexico City dotted with fountains, steel benches, and sculptures from the turn of the century.—Trans.

to talk to him. I had even told my wife not to hold up lunch for me. I wanted to have enough time for any unexpected situation. This just couldn't be: for nothing to happen beyond giving away a cigarette to a stranger on a park bench and hearing the word "thanks" three times. Who was he? Where was he from? What was he thinking about?

"Are you from here?"

"From where?"

"From here . . . from México . . . from the capital. . ."

"No."

He had stuck his hands back into his pockets. The cigarette was dangling from his lips. I observed how the ash kept growing as he smoked and how it fell on his clothes without seeming to bother him. Suddenly, he moved, he sat up straight.

I thought he was going to get up and leave me there alone, without my having been able to say anything to him, frustrating all of my useless compassion. I couldn't allow it. I felt I should speak to him clearly, directly, and without beating around the bush. I felt I should embrace him and tell him not to suffer; that he wasn't alone; that I was his friend and we were living on the same planet, at the same time, in the same country; that now the two of us were in the same park, on the same bench; that human beings should talk to each other, be aware of each other, and love each other; that each man who passes by offers us the chance for companionship and warmth; and that some people's indifference and disdain for others is a sin, the worst of all sins.

I felt I should say all of this, and I said it in spurts, gabbling and trembling with emotion. As I went on talking, I experienced the sensation that at last I had found the way. I felt that I was myself and at the same time someone else, someone else who was freeing me and reconciling me with myself.

I don't know at what point or at which word that fellow interrupted me. I just remember his hard expression and his icy, biting sentence: "I'm not in the mood for sermons!"

He got up and walked away.

I couldn't express what I was feeling. Now that I'm trying to write it down, after having revealed the great error to myself, I can say that my feeling was one of sadness and disillusionment, but at the same time, I felt that my pride had been wounded. I thought I hadn't been understood, that I had been cheated, that my goodwill hadn't been appreciated, and that, unfortunately, I had addressed someone who didn't deserve me. I felt superior. After a few minutes went by, I got up, walked a few blocks, and took a bus home. I watched the people who were on it: inexpressive, sweaty, drowsy faces. I admit it, I felt a certain repugnance.

When I got home I demanded my lunch.

"You said you weren't coming home," my wife reminded me. "I don't know if you'll like what I made."

"But I did come; I wanted to come home; I changed my mind," I answered harshly.

She just expressed her fear that I might not like the food. She didn't reproach me at all. I was unfair. I knew it and could do nothing about it.

As usual, she didn't reply and she didn't stick up for herself.

I liked the food, but I didn't say anything to her. I was thinking: "If they won't let me be good, then it's time to be rotten. Is that what they want? Well, that's how it has to be; a person has to be selfish."

And I was with the person who least deserved it. I ate quickly, locked myself in my room, let myself fall into bed, and closed my eyes so that they'd think I was asleep and not bother me. I didn't have to go back to the office that afternoon; it was Saturday. I don't know how long I stayed like that, pretending to be asleep while I was actually going over the scene with the stranger word by word. Gradually, I calmed down. I still felt, nevertheless, a great bitterness and was sure I'd never repeat the experience. I was thinking: "Of course, there was some reason I never dared do it before. It was better when I only wanted to; because then everyone, anyone, seemed to be the chosen one, the proper one, the only one."

I've said that suddenly I understood. I remembered the sentence: "I'm not in the mood for sermons!"

Sermons. That word seemed so offensive, so harsh when I heard it, and it explained everything to me now. Of course, that wasn't it, it just wasn't like that.

What meaning does the pompous, overly broad, abstract concept that all human beings should approach each other, speak to each other, and love each other have for a man, just one, for a shattered, wounded man who is trapped by who knows what kinds of problems and suffering? Perhaps he'll come to understand that someday. Perhaps. But the road, the easy route for him to come to that greater truth, has to be right for him, and the measure of one man is another man. Therefore, the words addressed to him should have been exclusive, dedicated to him; the name pronounced should have been his own; and the path should have been so narrow and straight that it would inevitably have caused an encounter, even if both were moving away from each other.

And what did I do? I can't forgive myself. He must have been terribly angry.

Maybe he didn't have anybody, not a soul in the world, and I spoke to him of everyone. My real intention was to offer myself to him, just myself, and then I bombarded him with a multitude of men, precisely those among whom he felt lost. And instead of reaching out my hand, mine alone, with its bones, its wrinkles, its unkempt nails, and its warmth, I offered him everybody's hand, which naturally must have felt like a claw to him.

And my tone! Speaking of love and fellowship in the tone of an imperative and fervent sermon, when to speak of love, of that pure love that isn't from one person to another but from one to any other, one needs a weaker voice and more modest words.

I shouldn't have said all that to him. Now, only now, when I've lost him and will never see him again, I know what I should've said. How different it would have been, for example, if everything had happened like this: "I envy you those shoes you have on . . . they must be comfortable . . . I can't stand the ones I'm wearing anymore . . . !"

Then he would have cast a quick glance at my new shoes. I wouldn't have said anything, but I would have insisted: "Yeah, they're new, but they're so cheap that the sole is burning up my feet."

With that, I would have created a certain equality between our shoes. His were old but comfortable and of good quality; mine were new but cheap and unbearable. And to emphasize that I was as poor as he was and that yesterday I was as much in need of shoes as he was, I should have said: "I bought 'em today . . . I had to put cardboard in the others to cover the holes in the bottom."

It would have been impossible for him not to ask me something, at least the usual: "How much did they cost you?"

I would have reduced the price of my new shoes considerably to guarantee their poor quality and also would have said I had bought them on credit from a man who sells them in the office.

This part is true. So when I said the bit about the credit, I could have spoken to him about how I manage to buy everything that my wife, my children, and my house need. And he would have found out, noticing it as if it had subtly slipped out, that I am married, have children, work in an office, and am poor—in other words, he would have found out about my life, about what my life really is. Because now that I'm writing this, I see that I can't say anything else about myself. I wasn't going to tell him about that, not a chance! . . . that I have this note-book I write in and the other one . . . the other one . . . that's still empty.

Oh God, that again . . . ! It seems like one of those knives whose blade pops out just by slightly pressing a . . . the shoes, that man . . . ! That's all that matters to me . . . ! What for? Not that either . . . not anymore . . . . What I want is to sleep and forget about the man and the notebook, more than any-thing about the notebook, more than anything about the notebook.

LORENZO IS SICK AGAIN. WHAT AM I GOING TO do? What am I going to do about that child? It's not fair, but sometimes it upsets me to see José so healthy, so tall and strong, because it seems to me that I'm guilty of poor distribution. We just gave Lorenzo a shot and bathed him so that his fever would go down. How weak and helpless he is! You can see all of his bones.

My wife is staying up to care for him. I'm not tired. I've drunk a lot of coffee and I feel jittery. I'm ashamed to be here writing, to be eager to write, but that's how it is. I can't do anything else—get drunk, maybe. But that's out of the ques-tion now. No, no, out of the question.

I JUST READ OVER WHAT I WROTE ABOUT THAT man the other day. The way I'm feeling right now, I just couldn't be that same person who thinks he can help someone else. Oh, I have such a need for just the opposite; such an urgent need to drop down on any old bench in any old park or any old bar and wait, wait for God knows what.

I write lines. I get everything wrong, everything ends up falling short, and, what's worse, everything has a core of arrogance and self-interest.

Who am I, for God's sake?! Who do I think I am to suppose that my mere presence and a few sentences will console a man who doesn't even know me?! Why, and with what right do I choose the privileged place of him who gives and put another in the place of him who receives? And it still hurts me that he wouldn't accept that fabricated brotherhood, that he violently rejected it. That's not true love for mankind. Neither is the eloquent sermon or the benevolent shoe trick. And what do I even know of true love? In any case, I feel that fraternity and love can't be planned; they simply happen and should reflect the ease and imminence of a common event in which one participates naturally.

Why didn't I approach just anybody, the first one who crossed my path? Why did I choose precisely that man with the miserable appearance and stern expression? I have to admit it was because I needed to please myself with the idea that I was helping someone who was suffering. In other words, I wanted to do something worthy of merit. Do it myself.

Why didn't I put myself in his place, where he was the one who gave and I the one who humbly accepted? Instead of my sermons or in place of the imagined shoe conversation, why couldn't I have said: "Forgive my daring, sir. I need to talk to someone . . . and I think that you . . . that is, if you wanted to . . ."

Perhaps he would have said he was in a hurry, that he had to leave. But, then again, he might have asked me what was the matter.

And to help him to help me, I would have chosen my simpler torments. I don't mean to say the smaller ones, but rather the ones that are easier to understand.

I wouldn't have told him that I'm a man trapped between four plain walls, or that I sometimes feel I'm being suffocated because I know by heart the number of steps on the stairs to my office; because I know the names and the voices and the footsteps of all my neighbors; because I've exhausted the possibilities of discovering new patterns in the stain on my bedroom ceiling; because every day, for the past eight years, I've run into a man on the bus who gets off a block before I do; because Rosendo Arellano comes over every month on a Saturday, without fail, to collect on the IOU for clothing I buy from him; and because every time the manager comes into my apartment and passes me, he says the same thing, exactly the same thing: "Hello, hello . . . my friend García, always up to your neck in papers!"

My friend García! As impersonal and indifferent as if he had said any number!

But I wouldn't have told him any of that. I never talk about it. Just here, in my notebook. I don't want to inspire pity in anyone. The pity I have for myself is enough. Besides, normally you can't complain about that. It's not a pain, it's not a misfortune. It's called stability, security, and many men long

for and even enjoy it. Well, how could I have complained about it? How could I have talked about those strange torments?

No. I would have spoken about . . . about what? Maybe about Lorenzo, his illness and our worries; maybe about José and the perils of his difficult age, the bad company he keeps and all those problems that young people have; or I might have said—yes, perhaps . . . that usually unifies men—that I had a heartache. I would have told him how I struggle not to go and knock on a door; how, when I can stand it no longer, I tremble as I dial a telephone number, listen to a voice, and bite my lips so as not to shout out a name; how I suffer from jealousy, that gnawing pain that burns a man's insides; how, despite it, my desire continues unchanged, alight on one body; and how, for that reason, the concept of the impossible has become the only one that I understand and the only one that I don't understand.

I know if I had made this up and told it to anyone in the park, he would have understood. Surely, he would have answered as they all do: "Forget about it, man. Let's go have a drink!"

And we would have gone into a bar where the empty bottles would have piled up in front of us. He would have assured me: "There's not a woman in the world who's worth a man's tears," and, "You've got to be tough," and then would have obliged me to write down an address. And I would have told him that he was absolutely right, so that he would have felt that his company and his advice had helped me and raised my spirits.

It could have been like that. But maybe the fellow in the park would have been a man who wouldn't have said what they all say. Then we wouldn't have gone to a bar to empty bottles and repeat the classic "macho" phrases but would have plunged instead into our own depths, into our own troubled places of pain where a man suffers the anguish of being a man, and, at the same time, that of not being the ideal one.

That one could have understood an impossible love and the thought that a man can die of thirst at the banks of a long-sought oasis.

With that one I could have spoken about how the peaceful, methodical, steady repetition of my actions smothers me, and how I am ashamed and oppressed by the knowledge of myself and the conviction that I will never have the courage to turn my back on that stability, that small order in which I live and make my family live.

Yes, I could have told that man: "I'm José García, you know? The dark, honorable José García who is destined for the three-by-six-inch obituary in just one newspaper: 'Yesterday, on such and such a day, Mr. José García passed away. His unconsolable wife, his children, and his sisters mourn him with profound grief.'"

Who will read it? José García died. Everybody will die and there will always be new José Garcías to replace them and occupy their minimal places in life.

LIES, ALL LIES.

The encounter with what I've written the day before always displeases me. With apparent modesty, I say: "José García died; who is going to read about it?" And with that, surely, I wanted to give the impression that I recognize my small lot in life and am content with it. And, now, at this moment a few days later, I'm feeling the transcendence of my death, of my own death, yes, precisely because it's mine. And I feel that I matter so much to myself that that interest must be shared by thousands, millions of people, who must be interested in and shaken by my death.

I also write, with false, with modest bitterness, that "any other José García can occupy my minimal place." Do I really believe that? No. I don't believe that. I don't feel that way. On the contrary, it seems that no one, no other man, can ever fill the empty space each man leaves when he dies. Precisely for that reason, in life, death stands still like a terrifying void.

Nevertheless, I always say what I'm feeling when I write, even though one idea may contradict the previous one. I'm a man with so many momentary truths that I don't know which one is true. Perhaps having so many is my only truth, but I'd still like to be firmer, more definite.

I've seen trees in winter, the time of hardship: naked, delicate, silent trunks. I've seen them in spring, covered with foliage, rustling, full of fruits. But all of these, the foliage, the rustling, and the fruit, are what is new and previously unexperienced, what is reborn each year. The real existence of the tree, its continuity and sustenance, are in the unalterable trunk.

Oh, I wish I had, at least, one idea, one belief that I could always go back to. I don't have even one hardened, permanent thought. They all fall from me into this submissive notebook, like provisional foliage, like thoughts "about the seasons." What good will they be? Who will benefit from them? Why do I insist upon writing them?

The other day I was thinking about this disease I am suffering from. It doesn't bother me—well, sometimes a little, but it's bearable, like fatigue. But with these heart ailments, there is always the risk of something sudden. I thought: "If I were suddenly to die one day and someone, my wife, my children, a friend, found my notebooks and was curious enough to read them . . ."

If José were the one to find them, he would feel let down by his father's "novel" and would probably tell his friends that I had destroyed all of my papers before dying.

If my wife were to find them, she'd keep them. Yes, I'm sure she'd keep them, the same as my pipe, my glasses, and my suits, and cry.

If, for some odd reason, I don't really know what it could be, one of my office mates happened to read them, he would shake his head understandingly: "Poor García, such a good fellow. Now I understand why sometimes he sat so still, as if he were numb, thinking."

And no one would understand why I couldn't tear them up, why I've never been able to, why at night I timidly approach them and take them with a tender but sad love and caress their covers, alarmed by the full pages and ecstatic before those that are still empty as I think that sometime, on one of them, I'll finally write something, I don't know what, something that won't have to stay in the shadows like all of this.

True, for some time now, I've been writing more comfortably. Before, I had to hide because everyone took me seriously, and that was embarrassing. But now, since my habit of writing has become "my mania," "my obsession," I practice it with a certain cynicism. When they respected me, naturally, they inhibited me. Now I go into my office with great care, with self-confidence, so that all can see me. Only when I have closed the door, taken the key to my desk from its secret hiding place, opened my notebook, and taken up the pen do I feel the anguish and the attraction of being on the edge of a deep abyss return to haunt me.

I wish I could at least explain what I feel so that people might understand why I write and why I can't tear anything up.

I speak of anguish, of attraction, of abyss, but these words don't reflect what I want to explain; they are clumsy, clumsy approximations. What I want to say is something different.

My hand doesn't end at my fingers: my life, my circulation, my blood extend to the tip of my pen. I feel a warm and rhythmic throbbing in my forehead. When I get ready to write, an urgent happiness starts to spread throughout my entire body. I belong completely to myself, I use all of myself. There isn't a single atom of myself that isn't with me, knowing and sensing the imminence of the first word.

I put a kind of sensuality into the first word: I draw the capital letter, accentuate its borders, and adorn it. That calligraphic sensuality, I later realize, is nothing more than the way to put off the moment when I have to say something. I don't know what that something is, but the pleasure of that absolute moment, full of joy, full of possibilities and of faith in myself, can't be clouded over even by the desperation that invades me a moment later.

Then I think that something, something physical, is missing. My pipe is filthy. I haven't cleaned it for several days. How can I write if my damn pipe is clogged? Mechanically, I start to clean it and, gradually, solicitous, compassionate hope again appears. Of course, that was the problem! Now that's more like it. A new, clean sheet would help, too. And slowly, once again, the elegant capital letter.

That is the beginning of what will leave me exhausted hours later. My body, which was going along with me so politely, begins to become independent; its toes start to hunch up nervously, a cold line runs the length of my spine, my neck aches, and the inside of my head feels like a spiral that spins quickly trying to find something, something that could express something.

And the only thing I can express honestly is that what I wish I could write is either already written in the books that move me or will someday be written by other men in notebooks that won't resemble mine in any way, that won't be so pathetically full, this one of impotence, and the other one of blank, useless waiting.

Full of the most difficult, the most painful waiting, one's wait for oneself. I've already had enough time to realize, to understand deep down, that I can't do it. So what am I waiting for? Why do I insist on keeping that notebook, in which I haven't been able to write a single line that's open, alive, and eager? I know it's waiting there for me. Its empty space obsesses and tortures me, but if I were able to write something in it, it would only be that, for a long time, I, too, have been waiting for myself, and have never arrived.

Perhaps that's why I'm always sad. I filled myself with an absurd confidence, founded on who knows what kind of vanity. Ever since I was a young man, I had made a passionate design for my life, just as I outlined a plan when I intended to write a novel. Outlines, designs, always the same thing.

First, I dreamed about being a sailor. I've already written about it here. It was impossible. One by one, I saw the ships sail away from me. I stayed on land; my pain was so great I felt that I was not on land but underneath it. Then, despite my fourteen years, I sought refuge by sinking my heart into a forty-year-old woman who caressed me almost brutally. She was my first love. I would have given my life for her, for her voice that, in the night, in the darkness, quietly and tenderly whispered the greatest obscenities to me. I'd feel my face burn for shame. I'd feel myself falling, falling dizzily into hell, and I'd try to stop myself by thinking of my sleeping mother and sisters who thought that I too was sleeping, not knowing that every night as soon as they went to bed and turned off the lights in their rooms, I'd jump dangerously through the window by the patio and escape, running without stopping until I got to her house, breathless. To "make me regain my strength," as she put it, she would give me a shot of liquor. She always made me leave in the morning. I'd beg her to let me live there with her forever. But she'd answer that everything she loved about me at night she detested in the morning. My youth was bearable only in the darkness. I went on cursing my age and adoring hers that had left in her dried-up skin, her gestures, her gaze, her words, and her round body an aftertaste of life that I sensed but was unable to understand or capture. It was as if she had already said everything that she would ever say to me and I was listening to only the echo, as if none of it had been devoted to me but was accidentally being lent out for a few hours, as if her caresses weren't born of her desire but of the casual encounter with my body.

I sensed all of that, far away, there deep inside me. And when she recognized it, she would try to make me forget by giving my small, inexperienced body the identity of a chosen and admired lover, capable of providing deep pleasure. And what she gave to me every night, she'd strip me of in the morning. When I was already convinced of my extraordinary qualities and our eternal love, that eternity was quickly shattered by a harsh, chrome alarm clock. At five in the morning or five-fifteen at the latest: "C'mon kid, get dressed and beat it."

I'd protest, overbearing, with the confidence and arrogance given me by the memory of the other words I'd heard an hour before. But my protest and then my timid and destitute plea were crushed by her sudden coldness: "I told you to get lost, and don't ever come back! I don't want to see you again as long as I live!"

She'd turn her back on me without saying another word. I'd get up, afraid and deeply hurt. In order not to be late, I'd dress myself with tears in my eyes without making the slightest noise. I'd roll up my shirt and my socks and stick them in my pants' pocket. Before leaving, I'd gather up all of my dignity and manliness, that manliness which she herself had praised hours before, and hurl a curse at her that would make even me tremble but would leave her indifferent: "I swear I'll never come back."

Since she wouldn't even answer me, I'd pretend to believe she hadn't heard me and shout from the doorway in the hope that an argument would ensue and allow me to stay a while longer: "I'll never come back! Never! Do you hear me?"

"Yeah, kid, I hear you just fine. Now get lost!"

Perhaps no other boy would have gone back, but I inevitably would that very evening, and I'd make her a gift of some of the tender, fresh bread that my mother used to bake for me.

IT ALL CHANGED WITH THE ARRIVAL OF THAT Dutch ship. A strong hurricane damaged it during its journey, and it had to be repaired. The crew stayed in the port for almost three months. A tall, blond sailor, who was always laughing and drinking gin, spent the nights with her. I, on the other hand, quietly cried alone so that no one would hear me, and I swore I'd never love a woman again.

Many years later, I ran into her in a tavern. I wouldn't describe her here for anything in the world. But the feeling I experienced made me understand that it is only in the body of a person whom we have loved deeply for a long time that we don't perceive the passing of time, and that growing old with that person is a way of never growing old. Seeing someone from day to day has a slow, compassionate rhythm. The people who live at our side always exist in the most immediate time: yesterday, today, tomorrow; and we can't see these shrunken distances; we don't see the effects of the passing years.

I realize that my wife has aged only when I see old photographs. And not even then, because they were taken in surroundings so different from the present ones and in such ancient clothing that I look at them as if they weren't of her, as if the portrait represented not my wife but a character similar to her. She's the same one who yesterday, seated in front of me, looked at the portrait and laughed at "that extravagant hat"; or the one who today urged me not to go out without more on because it was cold; or the one who will scold me tomorrow: "I told you so, you caught a cold."

Her aging hands, her eyes surrounded by wrinkles, and her gray hair don't surprise or displease me or make me remember the smoothness of her skin and her black hair of a former time. The changes have occurred so slowly and are so intimately tied to my own that neither she nor I has been able to notice them.

I think that the great miracle of sharing your life is not perceiving the brutal destruction, the annihilation of the body that you love.

I LIKE SHARING MY LIFE. SOMETIMES I TELL MY wife that a man should live alone, unhampered, so as not to weaken himself. But I say it to get her attention, so that she'll imagine that I haven't lost my restlessness, and so that I won't feel old, moored for the last time.

I really don't know what I'd do if suddenly, for some reason, I had to live alone. If, instead of her warmth in my bed, I were to feel her absence; if I couldn't protest an abrupt movement that wakes me up; if at midnight I couldn't get impatient and tell her to move away a little bit because I'm too hot; or if in the early morning I couldn't squeeze her hand and ask her to move closer. I don't know what I'd do if I didn't hear her constant complaining about the house or her periodic threats of leaving someday to see how we make out all alone. Yes, she says all of that furiously, and it makes the children and me laugh because the only thing we are completely sure about is that she will never leave us.

I don't know what I'd do if we couldn't go on together seeing how the objects that have accompanied us and been useful to us for so many years are slowly losing their color and form.

We have a vase that someone gave us when we got married. It is so ugly, so relentlessly ugly, that it served as a running joke for the first few weeks.

"Remind me to break that thing tomorrow without fail," I'd say to her.

"Leave that pleasure to me," she'd request.

Later, we decided that it would be the thing we'd smash during our first big argument. Then we forgot about it. José, who, when he was young, broke everything, including his own body, mysteriously respected that big, obvious, and tempting vase. Later Lorenzo used it for keeping all kinds of surprising objects that he played with for a long time: spools, chicken bones, fruit pits, nails, little pieces of wood, broken glass, corks, and who knows what else! Now, it serves its true function and my wife puts flowers in it when she can squeeze something from our budget and give herself the little luxury of decorating the house. Of course, it has never really pleased us, but it has come to have such a deep meaning for us, such an intimate character, like that of a companion, a witness, a survivor, that now we would doubtless suffer if it were broken by one of those calamities that we hoped might befall it earlier.

It seems we aren't aware of this and, in reality, that's the way objects are; they are simply there and age beside us. But, right now, while I'm thinking about them and writing about them, I am perceiving the importance they have for our love and how they protect and bind it together.

When we got married, I bought a kitchen set: pots, frying pans, ladles, all brand-new, magnificent aluminum. I was quite satisfied and very sure that my wife would be enthusiastic about them. But when she saw all of the shiny, new objects she said, with a note of anxiety: "Oh dear, I wish they were already old!"

It wasn't exactly what I had hoped to hear, but it was undoubtedly an expression of her good love. An expression of love that instead of enjoying the initial surprises and pleasures, thinks about what will last, what is permanent. Shiny and new, those pots were not yet ours. Once old, carbon-stained, and battered, they would be ours and their deterioration would reflect our fire, our food, our times, our shared lives.

And our children. That miracle that absorbs and lives within me. I don't know. It's something strange. Of course, I'm not always conscious of it. I deal naturally with my sons, just like any other father. But sometimes it happens that I hear them speak and feel inside me something like the echo of their voices, as if I myself were speaking and they were the echo. It's not a father's love; it's not pride; it's a strange physical sensation that disturbs and frightens me.

When José was born, my wife lived through the experience naturally. I'd never seen her so happy! She'd take the child in her arms, bathe him, change him, rock him, and speak to him. She'd laugh at me and say that I was in love with my son, because I'd stand in front of him for hours, serious, silent, just looking.

"José, please leave him alone. You're going to hypnotize him."

I'd stop looking at him and move away, trembling with fear. Not because something might happen to him, or because we might lose him, but because of having him, because he was there, alive, and because of having given him life in a moment that had nothing at all to do with him, since, then, neither my thoughts nor my heart was dedicated to him.

I felt guilty, I felt remorse, and I would think of man and his great solitude. I'd think that we come into the world alone, terribly alone. I'd think that if a man and a woman who love each other and touch each other don't feel that that moment can be the cause of anything less than a being, and if they can't accompany that being with even a flash of awareness, or love, or happiness, or tenderness, or terror, or pity, it means the man is born alone. And just as he is born, so does he remain and die alone.

Because everything that comes later is already different; the sum of causes and their effects, the incurable love for a presence that moves us, the natural care for a helpless one, the anxiety created by a cry, the sensation of standing in front of something of ours, something tangible that perpetuates our own existence.

I felt remorse for not having thought of my son, even for an instant, from within the whirlwind itself. I felt remorse for not having given him my awareness from that moment on, or precisely at that very moment.

But I wasn't aware of it, I didn't think of that during the long months of waiting that we spent asking ourselves, "Will it be a boy? Will it be a girl?" searching for a name, tailoring a little fluffy wardrobe of a specific color, and other such frivolous conjectures.

Only when I saw him and thought that he too saw me, and

only when I heard his cry, the cry that begins life, did I start to feel guilty. And to make up for the time when I had left him alone, especially for that second when I hadn't thought of him, I accompanied him always, no matter the hour. I looked deeply at him and within myself begged his forgiveness.

But, despite my exaggerated dedication, I already knew that there was no solution for any of it. He had been alone in his first moment, he had been alone afterward, he was alone now and would be always until his death. He would grow up and feel well cared for and loved; he would surround himself later with other beings whom he had chosen; he would himself love and have children as indifferently as I had had him; and he would die alone, as alone as when he was born.

Then, it really upset me to think about it. Now, I know that nobody can accompany a man in those two solemn moments— when he is born and when he dies. And I know because, as always, my wife, who knows everything that doesn't have to be learned, revealed it to me without realizing it.

One evening while José was crying, I asked her: "In those moments, while we were loving each other, tell me the truth, did you think of the child?"

And, as she came closer to me, she answered in a low voice: "In those moments, I don't think."

"I don't, either," I answered, so as not to make her ashamed of her love. But afterward, to make her ashamed of her blind maternity as I was of my blind paternity, I said deliberately: "Poor child!"

It was then that she immediately replied with conviction: "Poor child, if we had thought of him in those moments, I think he never would've forgiven us for the premeditation."

I felt as if struck by a blow. Later, I was struck again and I felt she was right. I then found out it was true, because it calmed me, and suddenly the path became clear to me.

From that night on, I could see my son happily. Because, of

course, it's not awareness but forgetting to be aware that opens the door to miracles. The slightest trace of awareness in that great mysterious moment would have been an act of utmost arrogance. And it's not arrogance but the ineffable state of grace, what has never before been thought of, total innocence, that allows us to endure the terrifying truth that we have given life to a conscious being.

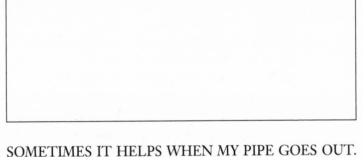

SOMETIMES IT HELPS WHEN MY PIPE GOES OUT. The time I use to fill and light it again forces me to reread the last sentence. This time I find myself with a sumptuous crowning touch: "the terrifying truth that we have given life to a conscious being."

For God's sake, for God's sake! Why do I insist upon writing? I should speak, just speak! When I speak, I never say these things. I do it with simple words that express my truths and my life, which is also very simple.

Writing is what complicates and upsets me. And it's natural, just that I still can't, or don't want to, realize that my only authentic expression is the everyday spoken one, the one I don't prepare, that comes out naturally: singing in the shower; the hurried "see ya later" when I leave in a rush in the morning; the abusive remarks on the bus crammed full of people; the slightly cordial "good morning" when I get to the office; the subdued "yes, sir," "as you wish, sir," in front of the boss; the usual familiar conversation during lunch sprinkled with those useless paternal reprimands: "finish that, Lorenzo . . . , you have to eat . . . , you're awfully skinny . . . !" or the polite praise for a common, modest dish whose only merit is the effort my wife took to give it a different look and taste by changing a few ingredients; or the "yes, I'll come home early," when I go back to work in the afternoon. And at night when the boys are already in bed, the daily review of our domestic problems: our sons' moods, their uncertain future, our financial difficulties— all of that in an intimate whisper that slowly lulls us until one of the two falls asleep and no longer answers the last words of the other, who, upon realizing it, turns out the light and in a few minutes also goes to sleep.

This is my language, the trivial language that is my fate.

And, of course, when I try to change it in this notebook and give it a different tone and harmonize it with reflections and questions that are categorically answered in my reality, I have to disavow and be embarrassed about what I write.

"The terrifying truth that I have given life to a conscious being" is only the pompous version of what I would say this way in my true language: "I have two sons, two sons who are slowly taking control of their own lives and excluding me from it; I'm afraid; I'd do anything to see them happy."

Yes, these are my words, and they exactly express my love, my uneasiness, and my willingness to sacrifice.

But when I am writing, the delight of composing a sentence, of finding an adjective, of rounding out a paragraph, distorts the expression of my true feelings; they are exactly like those of any other father, but, on that journey through what is . . . literary, we'll say, they lose their power and authenticity.

I understand that if I knew how to write, everything would happen the other way around: any feeling whatsoever would gather power and reach total clarity when explained or revealed. But I don't know; instead of explaining or revealing my feelings, I distort them with my zeal to write them down. I suddenly feel satisfied when I find the vigorous adjective *terrifying* and I apply it to the natural event of having a son.

If that experience were to seem really terrifying to me and if, above all, I were to consider strictly that "I have given life to a conscious being," I, a conscious being myself, wouldn't be able to live with it. How different to think the way I do when I speak as opposed to the way I do when I write! I've been nothing more than a blind, submissive channel—I don't know how nor will I ever know how—through which the breath of life slipped, leading to my arrogant son, José, and my pitiful, puny son, Lorenzo.

For that reason I suffered for some time, for wanting to have a voluntary role in this not terrifying but natural experience. I've already talked about it before. But now that I sense it so clearly, I don't know if I wrote the truth, if I truly suffered when my first son was born, or if that suffering was something I imagined in order to write about it because it seemed profound and suitable to reflect upon.

My desire is always to tell the truth here, in this notebook which is truly my own. But sometimes it happens that either I've forgotten the truth, or I think what I'm writing is the truth, or I write what I wish were the truth. When I look it over I find contradictions that I don't correct because I think, more and more each day, that nobody is ever going to read this and that some evening I'll have enough courage to burn it all.

On my birthday, I was on the verge of doing it. The idea that it was a heroic act, too heroic an act to be committed by me, saved me or condemned me. I forced myself to ponder what would happen if I saw my notebooks reduced to a pile of ashes. And I was afraid. Not because I believe what I've written might be of some value, but because I imagine that to burn it precisely for that reason, that is, because it's worthless, would represent such a splendid effort that I could never overcome the temptation to make a written record of it.

And I would have opened a new notebook and again have become its prisoner, lengthening even more the story of my sacrifice, in a notebook that, naturally, would have begun with a great lie: "At last, I had the courage to stop writing; at last I understood that I couldn't do it and bravely I tore up those notebooks where . . ."

And again I would beg everyone's and no one's forgiveness, for the relapse, assuring them that I was going to write just to remember the sensation I had experienced when I finally, once and for all, forever tore up my useless notebooks that were so cherished and so much a part of me.

ALL MORNING LONG, I'VE BEEN THINKING ABOUT the last thing I wrote. It's the truth. If I tear up those note-books, the thought of writing again to recount what I have done will haunt me. Well, I shouldn't exaggerate or give the gesture too much importance. But, on the other hand, I could do something less drastic, less heroic, and much more effec-tive. Yes, I think that would be a good idea.

I should keep them, and not write even a single letter for an entire year—well, six months would be enough—and use all of that time to observe myself day by day with utmost scrutiny and absolute honesty. I'll buy an ordinary little pad, like the kind they use in school, and every evening before going to bed, write down in it with all due sincerity whether my craving to write that day was strong, bearable, or whether I didn't feel it at all.

I'll sometimes allow myself to elaborate a little bit, as long as it serves the end I'm seeking. In other words, I want to find out, but seriously, scientifically, with statistics, how many days I feel good and how many I feel bad during those six months of abstinence. If it turns out that there are more good days, it means that I can bear up to it perfectly and that it's just a question of using a little willpower. If it turns out that there are more bad days, then . . . I can't, but I don't think that will happen.

When I say I'll be allowed to elaborate a little on the report, I mean that, on occasion, unforeseen, extraordinary things happen to a person that naturally alter the daily rhythms. When that occurs, it will be permissible to record the event and then to subtract that day from the total number of days in the final operation.

Because it's true: even though my life is very monotonous, something can happen that takes up all of my attention and keeps me from thinking about anything else. Therefore, if I don't make any note of it, I won't know with precision whether, on such and such a date, I had the desire to write or not, and in the end many days will be unaccounted for. This would alter the average and yield a mistaken result.

And I don't want to make myself vulnerable. Since I'm going to make the sacrifice, I want everything to come out exactly. Because it really is a sacrifice. I'm ashamed to write it down, but for me to make any decision constitutes a terrible effort. I lack character and courage. I've been like that since I was a child.

I remember what I went through when I had to choose one

of the many sweets that Mrs. Lola Urrutia would sell in that little box of hers decorated with tissue paper to "help make ends meet." They were made of almonds and shaped like fruits: pineapples, pears, apples, and oranges, tiny and made with true mastery. I loved them, but to choose one, just one, almost ruined the pleasure of buying it because, later, I was haunted by the idea that those I'd rejected were bigger and better. And Mrs. Urrutia was inflexible: "Look as much as you want to, but don't start fingering 'em all." Well, the one that I touched was the final, irrevocable one. I stuck with that one, but my desire lay with the others. I'd start to gnaw at it slowly with a kind of bitterness caused by that exclusive possession. But it was a sweet, it tasted good, and I slowly reconciled myself to it. It's always happened that way in my life.

It was the same with the suit that my mother would buy me every year at the beginning of December to wear for Christmas parties and later just for Sundays. What a torment! Later, at home in front of the mirror with the suit, I was so sure that the other one, that "little blue one" that my mother had recommended so highly to me, was the one I should have bought. I'd put the new suit on and go out into the street trembling, waiting for the compliments. It never failed that a good neighbor would say: "So José's got a new suit!" And although it was a mere observation and not really a compliment, that's how I'd take it. I'd smile and lightly pass my hand over the sleeve of that harsh, cheap wool.

And it was the same when I picked my first girlfriend at eleven. Next door lived two plump, blond sisters about my age. Their father was a German who frightened everyone with his deafening bursts of laughter, a good man who took life calmly and thought only of drinking beer and going back to his country some day. I wanted a girlfriend—on the coast all the boys have one starting when they are very young—but I didn't know whether to choose Elsa or Gerda. I liked both of them very much. In high school, I would hide away and write my love letter leaving the name blank.

"Dear . . .

"For a long time now, I've wanted to ask you to be my girl-friend and not to go with anyone else but me to the beach . . ." And other things about hugs and kisses. . . .

But when it was all signed and the complicated signature was drawn, the eternal wavering would surface: Elsa? Gerda? And the decision would again be put off.

And so it was postponed until one afternoon on the beach. Elsa wrote in the sand with a little stick: "Do you want to be my boyfriend?" And I only had to answer with the same little stick she put in my hands: "Yes." Then she ordered: "Write me a letter and declare your love for me."

So I did. Later, I found out that the day before, Gerda had received a letter like the one that Elsa asked me for. It wasn't that Elsa was interested in me but that she wanted to keep up with her sister.

That's how I met my first girlfriend, whom I will unavoid-ably always have to remember because of the letter "E," now faded by time, that I still have on my arm. I had the tattoo done and later had to put up with all kinds of questions. But how could I not have gone, like the sailors, to have the name of my first love etched into my skin forever? Luckily, I could af-ford only one initial. If I had had enough money then, her first and last names (Elsa . . . Elsa . . . Elsa . . . ?) would be dis-played, enclosed in a big heart. And this heart can no longer remember the entire name it once uttered at night, secretly, like a hidden sin.

And it wasn't shyness. No. It was eagerness. I wanted every-thing and wasn't willing to choose because choice represented only a piece of the longed-for whole. Now I think, perhaps very deep inside me, I foresaw that later I would have almost nothing of what I then wanted with so much passion. Perhaps I was defending myself from the mediocrity I'd later sink into.

But, what to do? Almost without noticing it or feeling it, life put me here, on the bottom rung of the ladder, where I'm trapped.

EVERYTHING I'M GOING TO WRITE TODAY IS THE hard truth. I'm saying this because it might seem like I'm cheating, and it's not that way at all. It's true the other night my pen got away from me a little bit and I wrote about those stupid things like the sweets and Elsa.

But when I closed the notebook around ten-thirty, I solemnly put it under lock and key and went to bed. I couldn't sleep, thinking that, starting that evening, the six-month period I had imposed on myself had begun. One o'clock rolled around. As is natural during those sleepless hours, many things crossed my mind. Since I was going to have the notebook put away for six long months, I tried to remember what the first sentence in it was. I couldn't remember it for the life of me. But the last one, since I had just written it, was etched into my memory, and I could repeat it over and over with precision: "But what to do? Almost without noticing it or feeling it, life put me here, on the bottom rung of the ladder, where I'm trapped . . . where I'm trapped . . . I'm trapped . . . ."

Suddenly, I felt something, I don't know exactly what. Something was unfolding, as if another man had stood up straight inside me, wearing some hard boots with cleats and walking nervously with long strides, trying to leave one place to go to some other specific but unknown place. I was uncomfortable and afraid because I felt that rough, grating character inside me. I remember I thought: "I hope he leaves, I hope he goes away as soon as possible. He's getting in my way, he upsets me." I also thought: "What's happening is that I'm nervous." I went into the kitchen, put some water on the stove, and waited for the first bubbles to rise. I made my tea and sipped it slowly.

A little while went by, but I still felt exactly the same: someone inside me wanted to say something, was saying something. Since I couldn't keep from hearing him, I tried to listen to him. But I didn't understand a thing.

I know I'm explaining all of this very poorly. Besides, I know I could simplify it and merely say that I felt terribly ill at ease. If I said it like that, everyone would understand. But that's not what it was.

Once I saw a painting in the window of an art shop: from a hilltop, a man and a woman, embracing each other with their backs toward the viewer, contemplate the landscape of their small hamlet. It is beginning to get dark; everything is enveloped in vague shadows. That's all it was, but I knew that after waiting for a while, it would keep getting darker, darker and darker, in the painting, and when night fell, the man and woman would take each other by the hand and go away. I was looking at it for a long while. Suddenly, as if I had awakened, I became quite embarrassed and moved quickly away.

That night, I also knew that if I waited for a bit, something would happen inside me.

And it did:

It was two-thirty. Without knowing why or at what moment, I got dressed and went out into the street without telling my wife. Our house is in a far-off, well-populated neighborhood, but at that hour there was no one in the street. Every once in awhile, the watchman's whistle would break the silence. I was walking without any destination, and I heard my steps differently. But I wanted to hear them better, feel that they were stronger, and I started to march in a strange way, with a slight military air, lifting my feet a lot, letting them fall with a thud at the same time that I was counting: one two, one two, one two. I soon became tired—I hardly ever walk, much less in such an energetic fashion. My legs were trembling and my heart was beating fast. "All of this is absurd," I said out loud, and I stopped. But when I heard myself, I understood that it wasn't and that I shouldn't lose that vitality for any reason.

I renewed my march. One two, one two. At last I came to the avenue, full of lights and noises. Grating jukebox music was coming out of a bar. I went over and, without thinking, as if it were a habitual movement, gave a hard push to the hinged doors that swung back and forth behind me. At first, I saw nothing more than a thick cloud of smoke. I approached the bar, threw a five-peso bill on the counter, and shouted: "A double tequila!"

Since the bartender was right in front of me, I didn't need to speak so loudly, but my tone must have been impressive because he served me a big glass right away, which I gulped down.

I ordered another and, with the idea of drinking it more slowly, looked for a table. They were all full, but that didn't bother me. I approached some grim-looking men with more of a challenge than a greeting: "Am I interrupting here?"

They looked at me with surprise. One said: "No. Have a seat if you want to."

I did. They stopped talking.

I thought of getting up. What was I doing at that table with a bunch of strangers? But it would've been so humiliating to walk off like that, to be sent away by an indifferent silence. . . . No. I preferred to provoke them so that they would at least insult me: "What's the matter? . . . Keep on talking!"

I can't explain why I acted that way, but at the time it seemed natural to me. And I really wasn't making any conscious effort, I wasn't playing any role. On the contrary, little by little, I felt more secure, as if I were assimilating that character who wasn't me but who ruled in me.

I ordered another drink. I only vaguely remember what happened next: loud laughs, deafening music, a woman seated next to me humming a song, my ID card being passed from hand to hand, a vendor of little celluloid animals . . . , that's all I know.

The next day I woke up in my bed and my wife told me that I had gone too far; some men who looked like thugs had brought me home drunk as a skunk, and, thank God, the boys were sound asleep and hadn't seen me in such a state.

She thought that, like the other times, I was going to stay in bed, silent, full of shame, and she'd be able to care for and scold me all day long. She was quite surprised when I got up, took a shower, and put on my new suit.

"Are you going to keep drinking, José?"

"No, I'm going to work."

"And what are you putting your new suit on for? Where are you going?"

I didn't answer.

I got to the office and went directly to the boss's office. Outside his door, I felt my legs weakening, but I exerted myself, straightened my tie, and walked in.

I won't repeat the whole conversation. I can't. I don't remember it well enough. I rattled off: "Sir, Mr. Andrade, you understand . . . a man can't stay on the bottom rung of the ladder forever."

He didn't say a word. He moved his head, smoked, and played with his pen. Finally he said: "It's true, García . . . you work hard, you always come through. . . ."

And he gave me a two-hundred-peso monthly raise!

My wife was astonished. I bought her a refrigerator on credit. It's not very big, but it looks so nice.

I WROTE ALL OF THIS DOWN TO EXPLAIN WHAT I said in the beginning: I'm not cheating. This was a pleasant, unforeseen event worth writing down. Tomorrow, I'll start counting the six months. Anyway, one day more or one day less won't really matter. And it was truly unexpected. If someone had told me that I'd get drunk that evening and the next day get a raise, I'd have laughed in his face. I don't know what happened to me. Maybe, when I wrote it, I felt ashamed for being in such a low position; maybe I was trying to forget about myself and wanted to show off a little bit among strangers. Or perhaps . . . could that be possible? No, then it would surely be cheating, but it's true that it just occurred to me. I wonder if I might have wanted to create an important, different event so that I'd have to write about it?

No. My resolution is firm, my sentence is six months, six months of complete abstinence. That's the only way it'll be possible to know if I can *not* write; if I can forget that absurd project of a book; or if I can humbly accept that what I love most in the world, what most interests me, the only things that console me for my failures, my smallness, my darkness, that put restlessness into my heart and joy into my life, are these notebooks that I'm giving up tonight.

But, I have to do it. During that period, I won't even open them so as not to be tempted to write. Perhaps, some evenings, I'll be able to reread them a little bit, change some words if I find a lot of repetition and, above all, something that has always worried me, check over the spelling well. I'm sure there are a lot of mistakes. I never learned the rules, and when I have some doubts, which is all the time, I write the same word with a different spelling on another piece of paper. Then I compare them and choose the one that looks better to me. But, of course, this doesn't give me any confidence, and perhaps the notebook is full of mistakes. I'll buy a good dictionary and, since I won't be writing, I'll be able to check over my notebook well, word by word, and assure myself it's all correct.

This reminds me of a failure of mine in the last year of elementary school. The teacher, Josefina Zubieta, with whom I and all of the other boys were hopelessly in love, surely had a great passion for sports because she organized competitions for all of the subjects, dividing the class into two furious, rival bands, a system that I now consider to be not at all good. We had contests for arithmetic, geography, history, and all kinds of other things. The supreme effort to defeat our adversaries certainly made us study, but what we gained in culture, we lost in fraternity and fellowship, because, if the group was made up of fifty students, half of them were our friends, almost our brothers, and the rest were irreconcilable, mortal enemies. And what our teacher thought to be a noble joust was not really one at all, nor did it end at school but in the alleys with stone fights.

I made my team lose in a spelling contest when I had to spell a word I've never been able to forget: *scarcity*. It was very familiar to me because I heard it at home so frequently, and when I went up to the blackboard, I wrote it quickly and with great confidence. Oh my! I think the vowels were the only thing I didn't screw up.

That mistake worried me for a long time. Once, I even thought of taking classes in order to spell correctly. But that resolution, like so many others, gradually faded away into the daily routine, where scarcity—since that day I have always written it correctly—of money, domestic problems, and all of those things have, little by little, cut back on my ambitions and my dreams.

I DON'T WANT THE SAME THING TO HAPPEN TO my sons. Since I'm no longer a young man, it's hard for me to picture them mature and educated, especially Lorenzo. Maybe José. Yes, he'll get married soon; he thinks of nothing but love. My poor son! He's suffering now because of love, that wild pain of adolescence.

Not long ago, I went to the restaurant where Margarita works, and, without my son noticing me, I observed him from a discreet corner. I don't know if I felt deep sorrow for him and cried for that reason, or if my tears were for myself, for my already-so-distant twenty years of age. The way his eyes followed her everywhere; the way they became soft when she passed by and grim and uneasy when she smiled at another customer; the way he'd look every other minute at his watch, counting the seconds until they'd close the café; the way he'd look at the door, fearing that at the last minute more people would come in and she'd have to wait on them! And what a face the poor fellow made when he saw me! I pretended to be absent-minded and walked right by him, counting my change. He quickly opened a book and pretended to read.

I didn't say anything to him that evening. I let some time go by and then tried to convince him that that woman didn't suit him. I timidly used the arguments that all parents use: she distracts you from your studies, you have to finish your career, you should look for a fiancée, a girl your own age.

How hollow it all must have sounded to him, how senseless, how weak in the presence of his stormy first love!

He listened without interrupting me and then, as if he were the old man and I were the young man, he said: "Father, you can't understand."

Maybe he's right. He feels I can't understand it. He considers my fifty-six years capable of conserving the memory of a twenty-year-old's love but not its richness. He feels that I keep the whole experience inside me, compact, sort of petrified, but that I can no longer separate and give the emotions their exact value that love aroused, that I no longer understand tears, hope, desire, or the absolute truth that the world begins in the head of a woman and ends at her feet. There are no other surroundings, there is no other horizon. She, she alone with her small boundaries that contain everything.

That's the way things are. That's how it was for me, too. I could say it to him and assure him that I remember it clearly. I could confess to him that I have stocked my life, my subtle, splendorless life, with those passionate memories.

But he wouldn't understand me, either. He came to know me when I was already defeated, stuck in my routine, and I've never given him the spectacle of a brilliant feat. I'm not my son's hero. I never could be. In the beginning, it seemed interesting and mysterious to him that I'd lock myself up to write at night. He was waiting for my book and, with it, for the father of whom he could be proud. A long time has gone by. He doesn't care anymore. Since he has his whole life ahead of him, he hasn't learned to wait.

I don't blame him for a thing. How's he going to believe that I understand him if I mention age and studies to speak of love? But what else can I do? There is a language made of years, of experience, which is the required one, the intimate and loyal one, which, nevertheless, comes out cold and dry. A wise language, the only proper one, which, instead of bringing us closer, separates us from those whom we try to protect with it.

I understand it and am ashamed to use it. My impulse would be to say to him: What really matters is whatever your feelings tell you that really matters. Don't pay any attention to my advice; experience lies at the end of the road, and I shouldn't deprive you of either the pleasure of the road or the sad wealth you'll find when you've come to its end. Because that's what experience is: a sad wealth that shows you only how you should have lived but not how to live again. I could protect you, but does my protection interest you? Throw yourself into your life, plunge into it naked, inexperienced, and innocent. And come out of it battered or victorious. It's all the same when it's over and done with. The important thing is the passion you've put into living it.

But, strictly speaking, can I, should I speak to him like this?

I'm always in doubt. The truth is, I don't know how to deal with my children. Sometimes, I'd like to become less doubtful and limit myself to imitating my wife's firm attitude.

I hid the relationship between José and Margarita from her, so that she wouldn't worry. When she'd ask me: "Why is that boy in such a bad mood?" I'd invariably evade the issue and answer: "His age . . . they always get like that . . . he'll get over it soon."

But a few days ago, a woman who lives next door rudely told her about everything. She didn't do anything I'd expected her to: no crying, no scenes, no tragedies. With great ease, she confronted and threatened her son in a way I'd never have dared: "If I ever find out you are still mixed up with that little tramp, you can just pack up!"

For her, that threat meant protection, even though it was a little fierce. That same sentence uttered by me would have sounded like tyranny.

Why? I don't know, but I think it's that she has the courage to feel like her sons' owner as long as neither they nor life itself shows her the opposite. I, on the other hand, feel like they don't belong to me, that I can't be so arrogant as to feel they are mine because their dependence on me is accidental. I can only speak to them with the fear that's aroused by mystery.

But she, direct and arbitrary, was the one who achieved what I couldn't have with my prudent, respectful intervention:

One night during dinner—Lorenzo had already gone to bed—José told us: "You'll probably be happy; I broke up with Margarita!"

I saw that his lips were trembling and that he was trying not to cry. I really felt sorry for him and hastily explained: "I'm not happy that it causes you pain, son, but . . ."

She interrupted me: "I am. Very happy indeed. I know it hurts, but you have greater pain still to come, José."

The poor boy looked at us with eyes full of tears. I was indignant at my wife's hardness and was going to say something to soften her words, but she beat me to it: "And you, you have yet to experience the pain of seeing a son cry."

And then something happened that left me out in the cold, as if I were a stranger with no business being among them. José

ran toward his mother and embraced her with such anguish
that it seemed he was clutching his infancy and taking leave of
it at the same time. My wife closed her eyes. I understood that
at that moment the two of them were far away from me, as if in
another world.

It was just for a moment because, surprising me again, she
dryly cut off her son's emotion: "Go now, it's bedtime; and get
out what you're going to wear tomorrow . . . you always end
up in such a rush."

"Yes, Mom," he said meekly, like a little child.

He hardly said good-night to me.

"G'night, Dad."

I don't remember if I answered him.

My wife began to pick up the plates; I was watching her. I
wanted to say something to her, but again, I was afraid to hurt
her. Finally I decided: "Do you think that José won't go see
that woman again?"

"No, of course I don't; what else am I to think? He'll look
for her first thing in the morning. The poor guy can't do anything else."

"But . . . what then?"

"I'll scold him again. There's really nothing else I can do."

Then, without a transition, as if nothing had happened:
"Finish up that coffee. It must be cold by now."

OF COURSE, HE WENT BACK TO SEE HER. I THINK it's useless to say anything. At least, I won't be the one to do it. I know he's not happy, that he wants not to love her. But if he can't leave her, why should I torment him, why should I make the situation worse?

Besides, and this is the truth, I don't have the moral authority to demand it of him. He doesn't know that I don't have it, but I know. My wife can lecture him on uprightness and strength because she is strong and upright. But me?

It happened five years ago. And it was totally unexpected!

I have a friend, perhaps the only really intimate one I have: Pepe Varela. He came to the firm after I did, and since our work was related, I showed him around a little. He thanked me for whatever I taught him with an expressive: "Thanks a million, buddy!" And that's how, indifferently, the way it always happens to me, we became friends. One evening, I invited him over for dinner. He hit it off right away with my wife. He's such a healthy, happy, and cordial fellow. The other day we went to lunch with him. His wife deeply displeased my wife. And I understood it very well. From that day on, she didn't want to have even the most superficial dealings with that frivolous, overly made-up woman who shouted instead of speaking and spent hours on end listening to the radio and worshiping her so-called idols.

"Bring Pepe home with you, but I don't want to see that woman again as long as I live."

He comes over frequently, gives toys to Lorenzo, and my wife advises him, scolds him, and pampers him. Pepe and his wife don't have children.

For their tenth anniversary, they had a party. The poor fellow insisted that the two of us should go, but my wife, who never would have gone anyway, managed to excuse herself because Lorenzo was ill. I went alone.

How could it have happened? I still ask myself. She was one

of Pepe's friends: a rather young, cheerful, good-looking, and ostentatious woman, a soldier's widow who lived on a pension provided by the government. At least, that's what she said.

It was absurd to think she was interested in me. I was fifty-one at the time and, as I've already said, I'm not the least bit attractive. At that time, I no longer worried about being attractive to a woman. Any bold compliment, any advance on my part, would have seemed grotesque to me. I thought that my desire for adventures had disappeared forever. I had my wife, whom I love serenely, and I led the normal life of those men who, if they're not over the hill (I did happen to have a two-year-old son), are tired and settled into their advanced age and resigned to it.

During dinner, she made obvious insinuations to me. I was surprised but nothing more. I attributed it to the several drinks we had had and didn't give it the least importance.

I remember when I came home, I jokingly said to my wife: "I made a conquest."

And she answered: "That's great. But tell me about it tomorrow because it's already late."

I went to bed and started to feel sick. I asked her to give me a little bicarbonate.

She got up and said with a laugh: "Go on, Don Juan! If your conquest could only see you with that expression on your face!"

I also laughed. And I didn't think about the incident again.

Two days later, she called me at the office. When they told me that there was a call for me from a woman, my legs went out from under me.

"Lorenzo!" I thought.

My wife calls me at work only when something serious happens: that time José fell and cracked his head open, when they told her that her father had died, the day the maid burned her hands with gas. Only for emergencies. And the boy had been quite sick.

But it was Lupe Robles, and she wanted to invite me to "a niece's birthday party."

I told Pepe, and he said that when I left the party, she had spoken very highly of me. And then, with his male appetite, he advised me: "I'd go if I were you. Anyway, a little fling never hurt anyone."

For the first time in years, I lied to my wife. My heart pounded while I was explaining to her, in more detail than necessary, that I hadn't been able to find a number in the books and was going to stay in the office after hours to check over several entries; that Pepe had offered to help me and, when we left, I'd have dinner with him somewhere.

"Come home if you want to. I'll have something for you both here."

"No. Who knows when we'll finish."

"Don't stay up too late, dear; you already work too hard."

I don't know if I felt mad or ashamed when I listened to her. Why didn't she suspect something and try to keep me from going so that I could get worked up, fight, and ease my conscience a little? I'd have gone anyway, but not with that sense of remorse. And I would have gone because there was nothing else that I could do. That call had awakened a dormant, withered region in me that had been numbed by my problems and my weariness. But it was still there, and now it was slowly stirring and trembling from fear and surprise.

A woman had come after me! I was going not precisely to meet her but to meet myself. She didn't interest me as a woman in a natural or erotic way but rather as the character who had sought me out, who had chosen me. This aroused so much emotion and gratitude in me that nothing or no one could have kept me from answering her call.

I wanted to do things right, to show that I was gallant and had savvy. Before going into the office, I went by a flower shop

and ordered a great big bouquet for the niece and a corsage for
her. When they told me how much it was going to cost, my
heart stopped, and I remembered my wife, saving, haggling,
counting every penny in order to "make it to the end of the
month." For a second I thought of canceling the order, then of
getting something cheaper, but I was embarrassed to do it in
front of the clerk, a woman I didn't know and would surely
never see again as long as I lived. Feigning great self-assurance,
I paid an amount equal to four or five days' expenditure in
my home.

I made them arrange the flowers right there in front of me
because I wanted to see how they'd look. They took an awfully
long time. I got to the office late and was so nervous I couldn't
do a thing. Later, I went to see Pepe in his apartment, and we
talked about her.

"Have a good time, but don't go and take her seriously."

"Why do you say that?"

"Well, why do you think, man?"

I didn't want him to explain further. Something, I don't
know what, made me change the subject. Maybe I was instinc-
tively defending myself so that later I could allege ignorance.

Pepe didn't let on about anything. He's not very sensitive;
he's just a common, ordinary fellow, like myself, and, in this
case, I demonstrated it more than ever.

Not only did I take her seriously, I fell in love with her like a
teenager. Why am I saying this? I fell in love like a fifty-one-
year-old man, inept and fearful. I was tormented by guilt, by
jealousy, by poverty, by the lack of time to be always at her
side, by the fear that she'd leave me, and, more than anything,
by the impossibility of leaving her. I'd try, would passionately
fight with myself with true tenacity . . . and I'd come back, I'd
always come back! What for? To put up with her demands, to
try to seem younger, to stupidly wear myself out following her

on her tireless pilgrimages to movie theaters, cheap vaudeville acts, picnics, fairs, trashy nightclubs, vulgar parties for friends, relatives, and neighbors.

I put up with all of that, which was a torture for me, only for her body in which mine was anchored without hope, without peace.

Many times, desperate, sickened by myself, I'd swear to her that I'd leave her forever. She'd laugh and with a frozen and confident voice would predict: "You can't. You'll come back. And on your own two feet, because I won't go looking for you."

And it was true. She would never look for me. What I didn't know was that I didn't look for her; rather I sought her for what she represented to me: my pursuit, my fleeting eroticism; my feelings of sinfulness; my vanity fed by the idea that I could still have two women; my anxiety; my last act in that troubled, male world of conquest, possession, and display. I held on to her, but in reality I was clutching all that would soon disappear in me. I knew very well that to leave her would be forever to abandon that underground, violent, grim, surprising, illegal, attractive, and yearned-for life with which we inferior men certify our virility.

I clung to her desperately, knowing it would be my last passionate act. I sensed that when that last mooring broke, I would again fall into the calm, asphyxiating routine, the everyday, rhythmic trot.

Sometimes, when her cruelty tormented me too much, I'd run home and feel that it was really my place, my only place. I would experience great joy when I heard my sons' voices, or when my wife, who knew nothing of her, lavished her habitual care on me.

"This is really what's mine," I'd think. "I'll never go back to that woman!"

And so I'd spend awhile dedicated completely to them, spoiling them, trying to make up for my deceit. I even thought they knew absolutely nothing about it.

But, little by little, the memory of her would rise up inside me: only slightly at first, stifled by my resentment; then with sharper definition; later, clear and complete until it became an inexorable order to go back to her. My wife would become intolerable to me, my sons would irritate me; I'd feel that the three of them were my enemies, like chains that hampered my every move. I couldn't say anything about it, and that made me detest them even more. I understood that the only way not to abandon them forever was to go after the one who was pulling me away from them.

I'd have to do it. I'd return conquered, begging, and start over again.

One Saturday, a woman who lived on the same street as our family and who visited often saw us at the movies. I'm sure she told my wife, because a few days later, when we were all having breakfast and I clumsily made up an excuse for having arrived late the night before, she stared at me and left the table without saying a word. But I never heard a word of complaint about anything.

Sometimes, I carried my absences, my bad moods, my getting home late to extremes to bring the whole affair out into the open. It never happened. I knew that, as far as my wife was concerned, I was guilty, but I think only those who have been in a prison, locked up in a cold, narrow cell, can understand that other prison in which the body, even though it moves around, is really chained to a desire that it doesn't want to feel.

I don't know if my wife's silent attitude was the right one. Without a doubt it was right for our marriage and for our sons. For me, for my desperation and helplessness, it was merciless. That's how I felt it.

You can listen to outbursts and even tolerate them. What's unbearable is not to hear them and to know they are there, stifled, eating up the heart of a woman who loves us and, with her silence, tries to keep us at her side because she knows that's where we belong.

I'd have given anything to hear one day her complaint, her cry, or her insult. I felt the urge to kill her when she pretended to believe that I was going to have dinner with the chief of personnel and said: "Put on your black suit; I've already set it out for you. You have to look your best."

In those resigned women, in what they call the proper attitude, proper for conserving the home, there is an unconscious and highly refined cruelty. Perhaps that attitude is convenient for some men. For me, it was unbearable, and it caused in me a pain different from all the others I'd ever experienced. It was a raging, embittered pain because it seemed to me that she was the one who was betraying me. I can't explain it very well; I can't find the words.

I didn't confess my unfaithfulness because I had to suppose that she was ignoring it; but she was already aware of it and deliberately pretended to ignore it; she was paving the way and forcing me to go on lying. And to match my lies with her loving attentions and pampering seemed to me to be the most elaborate kind of revenge. That's when I hated her with all my heart. That's the truth.

Then, I'd think of the other woman with relief and would hastily go out looking for her. I'd go over to her house and, without saying a word to her, would hold her, trying to forget everything that wasn't that desperate contact. But I'd immediately remember my wife, as if she knew her revenge reached as far as my most hidden intimacy. And when Lupe would propose, as was her custom, that to get us in the mood we go to have a few beers with her friends, I felt the urge to strangle her stupid joviality with my own hands and run home to my room, where she, my wife, the one who was mine, would be alone, silent, waiting for my return.

But I didn't do it. I ended up, as I did almost every night, drinking with her friends in a raucous nightclub, full of prostitutes, bums, and mariachis. All of that to score points and later ask her to go to bed with me.

I don't know why I insisted so much on it. I didn't really always desire the act itself; I'd even go into it with dread, and sometimes my fear was well-founded. What I desired with an overwhelming, uncontrollable urgency was her decision to surrender herself to me because, more than pleasure, I needed a title, the identity of a man still capable of having a lover; and precisely a lover who understood nothing of all this but who brutally demanded and was grateful for her satisfaction, the very way she did, or who complained when I didn't manage to give it to her, not due to any physical shortcomings but because "I didn't love her anymore," and "I was surely thinking about my wife," or because "I had other women."

Oh, how this deceitful, coarse language of sheets exalted me! And how the other one, also between the sheets, tormented me when I'd come home at two or three in the morning and climb into bed.

Many times, my wife pretended to be sleeping, other times she was really asleep—I'd notice by observing her breathing—but most of the time she'd wait up for me.

"Why don't you go to sleep?" I complained with exasperation.

"Well, I was asleep," she lied. "It's just that the slightest noise wakes me up. How did everything go for you?"

"Fine. Please go to sleep!" I answered dryly.

"Lorenzo got a little sick."

I blew up.

"What are you trying to say, that while my son is sick, I'm running around in the streets? Say it, go ahead and say it!"

"For God's sake, I can't talk to you anymore! Starting to-morrow, you're going to take something for those nerves."

In that way she deliberately avoided the issue and diluted our arguments with her boundless, energetic mothering, moth-ering that I desperately needed because fatigue and anguish were driving me to the brink of insanity.

This went on for two years. Pepe Varela, who absurdly felt a little responsible for it, went to great lengths to help me.

He'd speak to me in every possible way, with tenderness, with impatience, with brutal crudeness: "She's putting you on. . . ! I already know her! She doesn't love you. She's always had a man to take her out and to get her out of jams. The day you don't give her a penny, she'll tell you to go to hell and look for some other sucker. Try it out; tell her that for a while you won't be able to help her out. You'll see what she does!"

I listened to him and told him he was right, offered to do everything he advised me to, but what I really did was to ask the firm for advances, surreptitiously pawn my watch and my set of pens, ask for loans, accept private accounting jobs that I finished on the sly right in the office itself. All to give her some money so that what Pepe had predicted with such certainty would never happen.

It got to the point where I was completely bankrupt with no way out.

I'll never be able to pay Pepe for his generosity. One of his sisters, a hacienda owner somewhere in Zacatecas, lent him the money necessary to pay off everything I owed. Since then, I've been paying him off when I can, without his ever mentioning my slowness and lack of punctuality. I meticulously keep the account on a pad I hide in the office, and still, after three years, I owe him more than four thousand pesos that I don't know when I'll be able to pay back. Now, Pepe's set on the idea of opening an office by ourselves to take on private accounts from different firms. He promises me that we'll earn a lot more, but

I wouldn't dare give up my job without having something more secure.

One day, I did manage to leave her. I can't say forget her. Still, now, while I'm writing about it, the memory of her deeply upsets me. And it's not because I'm writing about it. No. The truth is that she hasn't changed at all, and I don't mean, as one might think, in my heart, or even in my body, but in some intricate, obscure cavern of mine where she's rooted and I haven't been able to yank her out.

She never found out why I left her. I said good-bye with the usual words. She didn't sense anything different about that moment. It's true that it was only a prolonged stare, but it was so deep, so direct, and, nevertheless, already so full of nostalgia, that I can't understand how she couldn't have felt that with it, I was trying to keep her forever in my eyes and that I was saying, good-bye, good-bye forever.

I found out that several weeks later she had asked Pepe why I hadn't come back.

"I told her you were seeing someone else," he said, beaming. "And now hang tough like a man. You've already done without her for a long time, don't go back."

Well, I never went back, even though I thought the only thing I wanted was to be close to her again. I left her because this world is made up of many worlds and hers was as uninhabitable for me as mine was for her.

Our only common ground was a bed I shared with my guilt, my desperate age, her youth, and her lies—with all of that, something only I understood and suffered from and only in one absolute, fleeting moment was able to forget completely.

It's hard, almost impossible, to explain what I felt that night when she closed the door that would never open again for me, because that's what I had chosen. I don't know if, when you die, your body lies there so empty of yourself, so lacking in memories, that you feel nothing, not even the vaguest recollection of fear, when the earth starts to cover it. If your body does feel it, I can say that that's what I experienced standing in front of her closed door, where I stood for I don't know how long.

There, behind it, was that bud of life, that passionate, sensual endeavor of mine, and that last possibility of turning away from the single parched and dusty road, to take the sidewalk that leads somewhere, who knows where.

I walked around for more than two hours. I was frozen when I got home and dawn was starting to break. I'm ashamed to admit it, I understand it's cowardly and childish, but what I wanted most of all was to catch pneumonia and for Pepe to go and tell her that I had died that same evening. I didn't care about my wife, or José, or even little Lorenzo. The only thing I craved was for her to think about me and suffer.

I turned down the hot tea and shot of rum that my wife, who was quite alarmed, gave me to bring me back to life. I had to give the pneumonia every possible opportunity. But I didn't even get a cold, which was one of my most frequent afflictions.

Exhausted, I collapsed in my bed and slept heavily for awhile. At nine in the morning, just as on every day, I got to the office, took the cover off my adding machine, and started to work:

14,312

976

1,345

The only thing different about that day was that before leaving, when my office mates had already gone, I took her portrait out of my bottom desk drawer and tore it to shreds.

The janitors were starting their 7:00 A.M. cleaning and, in order to undo that naive, heroic act that had obsessed me all night long, I'd come to my office early to pick the pieces out of the wastebasket one at a time, down to the very last one.

I still have it, and her face, crisscrossed as if by terrible scars, looks as if it was the victim of a strange accident or act of revenge.

How many nights, alone in this room, I've stared at it and a moment later gone out into the street, determined to go to her house! On the way, I regret it and return to confront my wife's interrogating stare, always with her lips closed.

Other times, I'd go to her house and stand outside, gazing at her bedroom window. The light would never be on. The most natural thing was to suppose that she had gone out with her friends or with some other man. But I needed to believe she was there, asleep in that bed of ours with that awful red, see-through nightgown—that I detested and she preferred—slightly raised.

At night, I'd go to bed with that image and a grim, sharp pain and dream of her, or not sleep at all.

Now, I'm more at peace with myself. She's still inside me, I've already said it, but so deep inside I feel her existence without feeling her presence. How could I explain this? I know she's inside me constantly because for her to appear with complete clarity, I just have to want to remember her, or have something remind me of her. That proves her existence. Now, if remembering her weren't a voluntary or casual act, but rather a permanent and obsessive one—in other words, one there in spite of myself—I'd feel her existence along with her presence. And in reality, I almost don't remember her. What I haven't forgotten nor will ever forget is my desperate love for her. I don't know if that's the same as loving her still. Perhaps it is.

IT'S TOO MUCH. I FEEL LIKE I'M FALLING INTO something I don't know how to describe, but it's not good, it's definitely not good. Later, I'll write about what happened, but to ease my conscience a little and to take a deep look at myself, I want to say that while it was happening (and, nevertheless, I was suffering along with Reyes, my office mate who was directly involved), I was thinking that I was going to write about it and that, in order to do it well, I'd have to pay attention to all of the details. So there were moments when I experienced both sorrow because of the event and enthusiasm for the possibility of describing it, and felt both with equal passion.

As time goes by, it seems that the notebook is becoming more and more a part of me, and it makes itself heard even in cases, like this one, where my moral obligation was to think of nothing more than the terrible conflict facing my comrade and long-time friend. It's not that I didn't behave correctly toward him, or that I've neglected him in any way. On the contrary, I did everything I could, just like everybody else, even something that required real strength: speaking out in public, in a courtroom in front of my own bosses, who watched me with rage. On that account I feel at peace; but deep down, I know I didn't completely commit myself because, at certain moments, I felt something like a hot wave rising up into my head and a sort of craving—yes, that was the feeling—to write down what was happening, to explain what I knew Reyes was thinking; to describe meticulously the movements of his hands, his agitated breathing; to transcribe his words with complete precision, and, more than anything, to capture and later be able to write down, without its losing strength, that moment when he changed his miserable life, his poverty, his anguish into a pedestal on which he stood up straight and silently stared at his accusers with pride and dignity. All of us from the office were deeply moved, but surely no one wanted, as I did, to write down the scene so that the image would never fade away: the image of that man who had suddenly recovered his dignity and value as a human being, something his social origins had deadened. I'm sure everyone else had focused his total attention on the problem; only mine was suffering from interference, from flashes of another problem of my own, where my friend—without his knowing it—and his conflict only had the function of providing me with a theme and a pretext to write. "I hope I don't forget to make a note of this," I thought when, harassed by questions, pallid, and with downcast eyes, Reyes took his handkerchief from his pants pocket, opened it up, looked at it for a second and, without making use of it, hastily put it back in his pocket again. It was obvious he had to wipe up the sweat that covered his face, but, without a doubt, he saw that his handkerchief was torn, and he didn't want anyone to notice. He raised his head and adjusted the knot in his tie with a certain pride. Behind that gesture, he was hiding his torn handkerchief, his suit with its tattered sleeves, elbows, and knees, his shoes misshapen by long months of continuous use; their life forcefully prolonged by frequent, ineffectual repairs.

While I was looking at his barely acceptable clothing, I thought of how we never make any comments when an office mate arrives with a new suit or new shoes. It's not that we don't take notice: it's that any comment related to the debut would be a tacit reference to what's been replaced. And we don't like to talk about those suits and those shoes that we throw out only when the state of their deterioration wounds our dignity.

I remember how ashamed I felt the day Clarita, the cashier's assistant, said in front of everyone: "Your new sweater looks so nice, Mr. García!"

My son had used it for several months, but when it shrank after so many washings, my wife had it dyed a more "serious" color and it fit me perfectly, since I'm short and narrow-shouldered.

The simple compliment, voiced in the most natural tone in

the world, scared me and made me think that everybody knew the story of my sweater, which is a common one in poor homes like mine, where an item is refitted and handed down several times.

I understood why Reyes tried to hide his handkerchief, which betrayed a poverty he had bashfully tried to cover up. That's why I'm ashamed for having chosen and set aside that gesture as good material for my story. That isn't right. My desire to write shouldn't seep out that way, in a surreptitious and hidden manner, and disturb me when I need all of my strength and potential to help someone who needs me. If it had to do with some event where I was simply a casual spectator, it'd be more justified, but this matter concerns me directly and, honestly, has hurt me because Luis Fernando Reyes has worked for a long time in my same department, and we've always treated each other with friendliness and warmth. We all really respect him. When the embezzlement was discovered, we couldn't believe it. He's a modest, methodical man, just another employee. He arrives on time, works hard, sometimes tells us something about his family, and buys things on credit like the rest of us. The only thing extraordinary about him is his good luck in the raffles organized by the girls in the correspondence section, who are very young and lively. Once he won some fabric. For a while, we expected to see him walk in with a new suit. Then he told us he'd sold it to his brother-in-law. Another time, he won a lady's wristwatch. It was about February, and he had the patience to keep it in his desk until September so he could give it to his wife on her birthday. It moved me, the way at the same time every afternoon he'd open the little velvet case, take out the watch, and wind it with a smooth, loving movement. Surely, he had never been able to give his wife such an impressive gift: around the watch crystal there was a circle of microscopic diamonds that glittered convincingly. When the girls gave it to him, he exclaimed, with great emotion: "It looks like a jewel, doesn't it?"

I remember that Rafael Acosta, who's now really acting like a true friend, told him: "The important thing is that it really runs well."

And looking at it with delight, he answered: "Oh, that doesn't matter; look how it sparkles."

Everybody laughed. I understood what he was trying to say: the function of the watch was to run well, what you expected of it, just as his and mine was to work in that office; but the fact that it sparkled as well was what was unexpected and, above all, unnecessary. He knew that the cold, exact, hidden machinery was not what was going to delight his wife, who surely had never had anything more than what she really needed. It was the sparkle, what was extravagant, useless, what had apparently been chosen for pleasure and not out of necessity, that would make the present different and valuable.

On the eve of that long-awaited day, a little before leaving, while one of the women under his vigilant stare shined the little watch by breathing on it and rubbing it with a piece of cloth and then wrapped up the little case "like a gift," he nervously and confidentially told us, as if we were his accomplices: "I'm going to tell her that all this time I was saving up to buy it and that I picked it out for her myself."

The next day, he came to the office with a haggard face. I thought the worst: that his wife hadn't liked the gift or that she got angry when she thought he'd spent money that they needed for more urgent things on something useless.

"Aw, you're crazy, García! She just couldn't believe her eyes!"

Then he explained he had stayed up late and had gone out drinking. The famous watch was the cause of it all. Other years, he'd given her common objects: stockings, an electric iron, a set of glasses. Since those things weren't anything special, he had given them to her in the morning while he wolfed down his breakfast. But this time, the gift was different and deserved a special setting. With several days' anticipation, he hired some singers, bought some liquor, and invited the neighbors.

"It ended up being more expensive than if I had really bought the watch," he remarked laughingly, as he squeezed his throbbing head.

IT'S STRANGE: DURING ALL OF THESE WEEKS when, for the absolute lack of time, I haven't been able to write, and just a few seconds ago, when I was scolding myself for having the desire to do it while Reyes was testifying in court, I was sure I'd write the story of the embezzlement with great intensity and detail. And now, after having written about that business of the watch, I don't know why I don't want to go into detail. I feel as if it's taking advantage of a friend, of a man's mistake, to provide pleasure for myself. Besides, it also seems to me that the details would soften, tone down, the story of an incident that's so dramatic it deserves to be written in a prudent, concise way. That's how I'll try to do it.

Luis Fernando Reyes, who has been a magnificent employee all his life, unlawfully disposed of five thousand pesos. That was more than two years ago. At the time the embezzlement was discovered, he had already paid off almost two thousand pesos at the expense of many deprivations the firm owners couldn't ever have understood when, trying to play down his offense, he began to recount them in a muffled voice in court. To us, the other employees, his deprivations didn't seem at all false because we suffer from similar ones; it's only that his were more extreme; but the owners insisted they were nothing more than "whimperings to awaken compassion."

That was when Reyes sat up straight and proud and refused

to say another word. He did the right thing. Our reality can be easily expressed: when it's felt and lived, it's strong and moving; when it's narrated, even with the most scrupulous restraint, it's strangely deformed and takes on the tone of an undignified complaint. Reyes understood this and kept silent, a silence that bonded us closely together and protected the only ones who could have understood that there was nothing undignified in his words.

Their reality is different, their language is almost foreign to us. We don't understand it, either. They think they're right; so do we. What hurts is to have to speak that way, about "us" and "them," instead of speaking about "everybody." What's really terrible is the importance given to superficial things, transitory factors that are superimposed, always added on to make up man's modifiable reality. They are precisely the things that finally distort what should be his unchanging reality, his essence and natural expression: love. If things were different, they would have been able to understand Luis Fernando Reyes, a human being just like themselves, and wouldn't have persecuted him so mercilessly.

When he applied for a loan because his wife urgently needed an operation, they replied that for that reason they made Social Security payments.* It's true; strictly speaking, they were right. He might have wanted to explain it to them but he knew they wouldn't understand that he didn't want to take his wife there; that the Social Security Hospital, because it was so large and overcrowded, represented, for Luis, a cold, impersonal

---

*In Mexico, many employers must pay into a fund to support public hospitals run by the Mexican Institute of Social Security, IMSS. Because of the difference in the quality of care, the doctor-to-patient ratio, and the kind of technology available, people often seek the services of private hospitals if they have the means to do so.—Trans.

place that couldn't receive her with the individual care he wanted for her. His case may have been like many others, though perhaps less critical, but it was his, and his also was the terrible fear of losing his wife, and his the anxiety of having to trust an unknown doctor who didn't know, and to whom it would have been ridiculous to explain, that that aged, disheveled, overweight woman was the person he loved and needed more than anybody else in the world.

I know Reyes didn't do the right thing, that he made a terrible mistake. What I don't know is whether under similar circumstances I might have done the same thing. How, then, can I judge him? They can because their reality is another one, so different that there is no chance they'll ever find themselves in a similar situation. But, in a certain way, we're no different than he is: we have similar problems and suffer from the same daily rhythm, the same weariness, and the same slight intermittent hope.

Surely this is why, and not because of generosity, we're defending him with so much compassion and are taking up a collection among us to take out a loan to pay off his debt. The firm withdrew its case, and Reyes was set free.

Now he's out there, free, desperately looking for a job where they don't ask for letters of recommendation. While he searches, he goes here and there, free, pawning and selling everything he owns.

As a matter of fact, he told me that in El Monte de Piedad,* they gave him one hundred forty pesos for that watch of his. It's still brand new because his wife never found an occasion solemn enough to make her want to show it off.

The Reyes matter had me tied up for more than three weeks.

---

*El Monte de Piedad is a chain of state-run pawnshops in Mexico City and the rest of the Republic.—Trans.

I really wanted to write about it, I've already said that, but I didn't have the time. I'd come home late, worried, and nervous and tumble into bed.

This makes me think that the best formula for not writing is to get involved with others, take interest in them, live their problems with intensity. Of course, it's true that I'd feel the overwhelming need to write about them, but anyway, it'd be better because I'd write something new, alien to me; something more than constantly tracing circles around myself and my own personal conflict about whether to write or not. Sometimes it seems that I'm on the verge of dealing with matters in which I don't participate or, at least, of which I'm not the center. In the end, I always wind up with the same old story. If I had the courage to check over the whole notebook, I'd come to this shameful conclusion: it always deals with me, my wife, my children, my house, my job. Always what concerns me, what matters to me. Always the same thing, like a cow chewing its cud. I think, precisely for that reason, I've been unable to begin the book. I've filled up page after page just to say that my world is shrunken, bleak, and gray; that nothing important has ever happened to me; that my mediocrity is total and self-evident. All of this, summed up here, explains only why I can't write something that will interest everybody.

Whoever might read this entry, as well as the entire notebook, could think I'm a modest and sincere man who's humbly confessing his impotence. But I now think these apparently modest declarations are full of arrogance.

Why, instead of writing to show I'm a mediocre man and shouldn't write for the public, don't I try to write something about what I and others like me enjoy? Why not have the modesty to limit myself to speaking about those unimportant things that distract us and help us to forget our averageness? I enjoy reading, and those who are like me must like it, too. But, honestly, I don't think that either they or myself would be interested in reading the book I dream of writing because I want to say something different and earth-shattering to everyone else. Perhaps we wouldn't even understand it. And, furthermore, isn't it true that I exclude the common men, those millions of men whom I resemble, when I say "the public"?

It's true my initial plan of writing a novel has failed, but it's also true that day by day my plan to write the book I'm so concerned about writing is failing.

Since despite everything I insist on filling up pages, why don't I make an effort to write a pleasant, insignificant story that everyone will like, those like myself—we who are fed up with our jobs, fed up with always leading the same life, who look for those light, simple books that help us forget all our worries?

I already know a novel is a very difficult venture, but I might be able to write a short story, an amusing anecdote about an interesting event that could command the reader's attention. Precisely this Reyes business could have provided me with a theme, if I'd wanted to relay it with all its details. The stage, a criminal court, is different from the already exhausted setting of my house and my office. Even though he's presently a friend of mine, I'd have the character talk about that time before I knew him, about his prior life, about the circumstances that favored his entrance into the firm where the two of us now work, and so forth, leading up to that terrible moment when he took the money that didn't belong to him. Then, and since it's always convenient to add a more profound crowning touch to the simple narration of events, I'd make some observations about how an act that takes place in a single moment, for reasons belonging only to that moment, can stay with us permanently and haunt us for the rest of our lives. The underlying circumstances disappear, never again to be present, everything changes, gradually falling behind us, everything slips into the shadows, but that one act stays beside us, keeping pace with us, walking hand in hand with us all the way to our graves.

Reyes will never be able to forget the moment when he took that money. He didn't have to look for his punishment in prison or in the unemployment lines, and it won't plague his conscience because he knows there were extenuating circumstances for his mistake. His true punishment is his memory, which will meticulously relive the event at any given moment, with all its painful details.

But, as well as being his greatest punishment, memory can also be man's warmest refuge and his most abounding wealth. For my new and more modest goal of writing short, easy pieces, I should call on it, just as if it had something to do with that aged box we decided to open one day. I remember perfectly my grandmother's languid, endless, poetic stories. I remember the sailors' nostalgic narrations sprinkled with foul language, which I interpreted as a symbol of manliness and later generously blended into my vocabulary. The scolding and punishments didn't matter; the important thing was to talk like a man and be tough with the women. I'd soon have them in every port, and I had to begin to act like a real sailor. I remember my Uncle Agustín's lavish tales. In his mouth the most trivial anecdote swelled to the size of a heroic feat, especially when he had a major or minor role in the event.

Yes. I've decided. For a couple of weeks, I'm going to remember instead of writing. It'll be a different approach. And right now, when I'm getting myself ready for it, I can already feel I'm going to like it, that it'll be something like a trip; not like the awe of being before the unknown, but rather like standing next to what you've newly found. I won't be besieged by memories, as usually happens. It'll be the other way around, and every night I'll get ready to launch into them in the same way I now get ready to write.

I know the search for memories, the way they appear, and the memories themselves have innumerable hues and forms. It's impossible, at least for me, to capture and describe their variety and subtlety. I can only say what happens to me. When a memory comes to me by itself, without my bringing it on, it arrives summarized, dense, and compact. Once it's here, I retain and expand it with the details that belong to it but that didn't come along with it when it unexpectedly appeared. Now, I won't limit myself to waiting for them or retaining them but will cause them, go out in search of them, and go over them carefully with all their details and relationships.

And then I'll write them down. But I'll write for those who are like I am, those who'll never be able to write a book that's for everybody. It's possible—and why not?—that after a certain period of training with short narrative, I'll acquire spontaneity, confidence, and even a certain agility that'll encourage me to come back and try again. A book can't be easily written. If I'd started earlier, if I hadn't wasted twenty years by holding back my impulse because of a vain and ambitious scruple, perhaps I already would've been able to write it. Perhaps what I need isn't imagination but daring.

I don't know. I don't know anything anymore. I'm awfully tired. The best thing is to abandon everything, to forget it all.

I'VE BEEN SITTING IN FRONT OF THIS PAGE FOR an hour without daring to pose the question. I really should. Do I still believe in the book? I often ask myself. There are times when I think I could somehow benefit from what I've written if I made a rigorous selection. But I'm afraid to read it because I know there's no continuity to any of it. How am I going to give it any order? Unless my character becomes thought itself, in all of its splendid, unbounded liberty, I can't see any way to stitch something together from all of this.

Besides, up until now I've done nothing more than talk about myself, which, in the beginning, was exactly what I swore I wanted to avoid. Now I understand I didn't have the slightest idea of my real possibilities. On the one hand, I recognize that I don't have imagination; on the other, it seemed illegal to take advantage of what had already been created and limit myself to pouring it out into my notebook. I also explained that I couldn't write about any part of my life because nothing especially noteworthy had ever happened to me; likewise, I declared I was attempting to write a book that would interest everyone, each page of which couldn't go by without the reader's hand trembling with emotion. All of that!

José García, read your notebook, erase those absurd and presumptuous words, and substitute for them the only thing that is really possible for you to sign your name to: "I can't keep from writing." Confess that your need to do it is stronger than you are; forget your farfetched ambition to write a book that will interest everybody; accept your true limitations and understand that if you haven't written anything else it's because you can only speak of what is yours: the memories that please, move, or wound your heart, the gloomy events of your daily life, and your relationship with a few human beings who coincided with you in your tiny orbit. That's the only thing that belongs to you, the only thing you can understand, and therefore, the only thing you can express. Maybe someday you'll manage to invent something. What you won't invent is the emotion that the experience probably would've produced in you had you really lived through it. Even though you derive it from the most pathetic, heartrending one you can invent, you'll never be able to put the warmth or the truth into an imaginary pain that you might etch into a story about a sad experience that is truly yours.

Strictly speaking, the only thing you can talk about is your own reality. And if you can't draw from it what you need for a different, meaningful book, then give up your dream. And if you can't keep from writing, then go on doing it in this notebook and then in another and in another, always secretly, until the day you die.

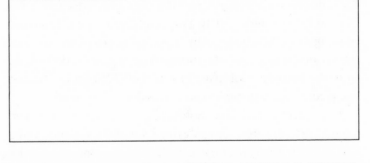

I HATE TO LECTURE MYSELF WHEN I WRITE. Such authority! Such a resounding, pompous tone! So many obvious arguments, so much stammering just to tell myself I'm not a writer, I'm not an artist, that I can't perform the miracle of creating another reality or of sublimating the already existing one. I already know that. But I do have the right to say what I think I should do, what I know I should do, even though I probably can't do it. In the final analysis, that's man's condition, the constant struggle between his yearning for perfection and his own weakness.

There's the trap again. I shouldn't shield myself with a truth that doesn't apply to the situation. It works in another sphere where good struggles against evil, but not here, where all that matters is to write something important or not to write at all. Perhaps good writing springs from intelligence and not from the conviction of what's important or from one's perseverance in the ambition to write well.

I know very well, and have always known, that I'll never say anything important and, for that reason, have held out for such a long time. I also know that I'll keep on writing in spite of it. From now on, my effort should be applied only to overcoming my yearning to be read, to see my name written on every page, to hear people say: "José García's book."

I know I can wage this battle and win it because it happens in an intimate place susceptible to improvement.

I know it'll be difficult for me. I know I won't open my notebook anymore with the same happiness as before, but will close it every evening—not with the sensation of having written in it but of having buried my words there. I think of this, and it seems that I, too, die along with my words. They've accompanied me and I them for many years. At first, they lived only in my thoughts, and all my efforts were aimed at muffling the temptation to write them down, but the time came when it was impossible for me to hold them back and they gradually won their independence. I've written about some things and brought up some memories. They've helped me to confess this obsession to write that is always gnawing away at me and have been useful for expressing my remorse for doing it despite having nothing to say. And here they linger, one after the other, in this hidden notebook. Neither my wife nor my children nor even a friend has ever read a single line. So many times, enthusiastic because of some idea, I've wanted to discuss it with someone, to ask for help, encouragement, or companionship! But who can I talk to? My wife tolerates my writing the way she tolerates everything I do, but she isn't the least bit interested in it. She says I could be using that time to learn English, which is very necessary nowadays. She may be right. But I can't blame her. Here, I speak of my frustrations, of my weariness, of my dreams. And she? Maybe she wanted, as I once did, a more intense life, or simply a more comfortable one. She's shared mine without ever complaining. She must also be tired of her own monotonous days, of the endless drudgery, of seeing the years go by. We get older and our children grow up and nothing ever changes. Nothing ever changes, nothing. What have I given her? Not even the hope that some day things will change, because I, too, have lost hope. How can I expect her to take interest in a book that even I don't believe in anymore? Even if she were to ask me to, how could I show her a heap of pages in which I do nothing more than contradict myself or debate with myself the possibility of my writing and my right to write? And this is why—she'll say and be absolutely right—you lock yourself up every evening and demand not to be disturbed? She'll never be able to understand that I just can't do anything else. I don't have the right to blame her or to ask her to understand me. But the thing is that she'll never read my notebook or know anything of the unyielding pleasure and pain my writing gives me.

There was a time when I thought I could talk this over with José. At first, he'd ask me about the book and want me to tell him "more or less how the plot went." What could I have told him? Then, he gradually lost interest, and now he never makes even the slightest remark about the book. I can't blame him, either. What's more, he's a radiant twenty-year-old and that's almost too much for him. He wants to fall in love, travel, get a car, earn lots of money, become famous. His exuberance, his eagerness, and his desire to acquire things get on my nerves. Why is he going to waste a minute of his time reading a few lines that have no plot and no thrills? And how am I supposed to expect him, who is on the threshold of everything, to be interested in me, who never crossed the threshold of so many things? No, I should never show him what I write, even if he were to show some desire to read it. He should never find out that life can trap us and, day by day, gradually narrow the broad roads we once dreamed of traveling on. He shouldn't find out that a twenty-year-old's dreams can go on being dreams for the rest of his life, and that there's no memory from reality that can be added to the memory of those dreams. His strength today wouldn't understand that my strength yesterday—which was so much like his own—wasn't enough to overcome all the obstacles. He'd only stress the failure of my notebook and would judge it by his age, by that age that's sure of overpowering everything in its way because along the way it ignores the many pleasing, urgent, and inevitable things we must willingly give in to. Those are the things that later will make us think with nostalgia of our youthful dreams; but if our youth could be returned to us, not by itself, but with the memory of what we'd lived, we'd eagerly travel along the same road to reach the arms of those memories that overpowered us so completely and intimately, to those we felt we belonged to. José can't understand this yet, and honestly, I find his raucous ambition somewhat appalling. Of course, it's his age. I understand it only too well, but I dreamed of an old ship, of valiant and generous deeds, and he dreams of having money and the latest-model car. The days when he was suffering because of Margarita were when I felt closest to him. I almost wish they hadn't ended so soon, so that I could have comforted him. But it's all over. Now he laughs at "that foolishness" and ardently pursues a rich girl who is playing hard to get. No, my son José can't join me.

Nor can my friends, not even Pepe Varela, whom I love dearly. Our work is the same, our problems very similar, but he has never thought that his life could've been different. The only thing he wants to change is his financial status; he's happy with everything else, which he never mentions. The evening I talked to him about my notebook, we were in a bar; the drinks increased my affection for him, and I felt the need to share my intimacies with him: above all, that very deep, very lonely one—my notebooks. But I'd hardly started to speak about them when I felt a cold wall separating us, and I felt that he, who was so good and generous, so careful with my life and our friendship, could never understand an obsession he himself was incapable of suffering from. I can't blame him, but he can't join me, either.

With my other work mates I maintain a friendship that, although it's not exactly superficial because the daily dealings imperceptibly tie us together and make us interested in our mutual and similar lives, isn't deep enough for me to dare to bother them or bore them by describing a conflict that's alien to them. It's so embedded in me that it would hurt me to hear it talked about in a banal way.

If only my Lorenzo weren't still so small! He too hides in the most inaccessible corners of the house and spends hours on end absorbed, fascinated, by who knows what. He, too, has and hides several pads on which he draws the animals he has created. One day when I was sick, he came into my room, sat on the edge of my bed, and told me that if I didn't tell anybody else, he'd show me his animals, and he told me each one's name. The pain his youth caused me kept me from answering: "And if you don't tell anybody, I'll read you all of these pages that I haven't been able to keep from writing. . . ." But, what will have become of me when he's old enough for me to be able to say this to him? And, above all, what on earth will have become of him? Will he preserve his fantasies, his reserve, his silence, and his ability to be amazed by the things that others don't even perceive? Will he still consider me worthy enough to show me what he imagines and gives names to? I'd give anything to have Lorenzo be my first son! I see time as a dramatic abyss between him and me. He's the only person who could accompany me in this particular solitude. If I die before he's old enough to understand my notebooks, I'll leave them to him. When he comes to these lines, he'll know he could've been the only witness of this secret part of my life.

But I may live a few years longer, and maybe he won't change too much. I've never put such fervent hope in anything!

I REALLY DON'T KNOW WHAT WOULD BECOME of a man if he didn't have layered within him other hidden, adjacent, makeshift men who not only don't destroy his personality but shape it by broadening it, echoing it, and making possible its adaptation to life's most varied circumstances.

I know there are strong, unbending people who choose a path and go along with a steady pace, without faltering or dropping their gaze from a fixed point. They're people who know what they want; who clearly set forth their views and never contradict themselves; who can repeat or sign what they said or wrote years before because it's still valid for them.

If someone were to edit my notebook and ask me to endorse certain pages, I'd say no. Nevertheless, I would endorse the notebook as a whole because, even though it's sketchy, clumsy, and sometimes even contradictory, it contains my ideas, my emotions, my life's events. Maybe it doesn't interest anybody, but it expresses me in my totality. On the other hand, when it's dismembered, it not only doesn't express me but slanders and betrays me, because each of my truths is no longer a truth if it's deprived of its relationship to the others.

It seems as if I'm always justifying myself for writing something I have to deny a few pages further on. It's true, but what can I do?

My first considerations were more serious and less personal. I declared that you shouldn't write when you're aware that you can't say something that's important to other people. I still think that's true. But one fact remains, a fact that I have to confront: in spite of my categorical, deeply felt declaration, I haven't been able to keep from writing.

I can't live on only my cold truths, on the concepts I can synthesize in three lines. I must also live on my weaknesses, my dualities, and admit that those three logical, upstanding lines that faithfully reflect me in a given moment can become, on another not-very-distant occasion or in a complicated and turbulent mood, meager or narrow or painful, without ever ceasing to be true. Above all, I'm not imposing this on anybody. I'm simply saying it with the same lack of meaning and purpose but with the same uncontrollable impulse and the same delight with which a child leans out over the curb of a well, shouts out his name, and is thrilled to listen to the way that mysterious cavity repeats it. He doesn't shout it for anybody; nobody repeats it. He himself shouts it, he himself listens to it, but his name has been tossed into the depths from which it returns with a solemn, telluric tone so different from that tone with which it was uttered that it seems to him not an echo but an answer or a supernatural beckoning. He then begins a dialogue with the black void and shouts his name again, and then phrases, which get longer every time, and, deeply moved, he listens to the echoes carefully.

I write and read myself what I've written. I'm alone when I

do it, but I feel accompanied, split in two. When I'm guilty of inconsistency, I begin a dialogue with myself and, with great surprise, I listen to the answer that emerges from my most hidden depths, from that part of myself I was unaware of that speaks out when it's touched off by a declaration or a goal of mine that it rejects or can't comply with.

My broken promises, my changed opinions, my conflicting emotions, all of my contradictions seem less serious when I simply think or speak of them. Thought and oral expression have a transitory essence that doesn't compromise a person. What gives an impression of informality and inconsistency is the frequent correction of the concepts recorded in writing, supposedly the fruit of long and conscientious meditations, or the meditation of a truth that seems indisputable to us. We affirm this truth with the same determination with which, days later, we'll endorse another that negates the prior one.

For that reason, and even at the risk of seeming inconsistent, I have to amend what I wrote hardly two or three weeks ago.

Lorenzo can't join me, either. I don't want him to know only my notebook. It's a book, my book, that I'd like to put in his hands with pride. I clearly felt it when he told me secretly during a party we had for him the day before yesterday to celebrate his eighth birthday: "Dad, do some magic because I told the other kids you were a magician."

Surprised, I reacted with great misunderstanding—even impatience: "What do you want me to do? I'm no magician!"

He stood still, looking at me aghast: "You're not?!"

My son's eyes and his biting question, a mixture of astonishment, disbelief, pain, disillusionment, and I don't know what else, gave me an indescribable jolt and a feeling of gratefulness so intense it almost hurt.

My son thought I was powerful and had made the other children expect something exceptional from me.

Naturally, I did it. I've never seen Lorenzo so pleased.

The house was a total mess. We took all of the cooking utensils to the living room to organize the most rowdy, exasperating orchestra imaginable. Despite my wife's protests, we dragged a mattress out onto the house's dingy, flat roof in order to execute several acrobatic feats safely, which of course activated that terribly bothersome heart flutter that I hadn't felt for such a long time. Rummaging around in all of the drawers and grabbing everything I thought would be useful, I put together six different disguises for Lorenzo that amazed his friends and made him feel like the most important person in the world. I left the Gang of Tigers formed and functioning and gave each child his rank, identity, and task. Since Lorenzo was the one to turn eight, he was designated the Supreme Tiger and immediately struck a commanding pose, smooth but firm, which surprised and greatly pleased me.

I was sure that when we were alone, he would hug me and thank me for not having made him look bad. Later, I understood that if he had done that, it would have ruined everything. For him, I hadn't pretended to be a magician. I was a magician, and he had no reason to thank me for it. He didn't hug me or make the slightest hint about the effort I put forth or my success. He confined himself to asking me how long it would be before his next birthday and saying good-night with the savage gesture I'd suggested so that he and the other tigers in his gang could identify each other. And with great dignity and solemnity, he walked to his room with a studied slowness.

I sat there pondering. He's such a slight, silent, imaginative child! He knows how to play and tell stories, to keep quiet in the presence of insects, and to keep his eyes open in the dark. He doesn't like regular toys; he prefers those plain objects he can mold to his fancy, just by saying so. His most extraordinary creation is a metal tube painted white. Quite naturally, he told me that during the day it's his friend named Riqui and at night it's his brother named Micaelo García. A while ago, I asked him the reason for that duality, and he answered that if Riqui weren't to come back, Micaelo would have to go to Riqui's house every night to sleep. And that since he loved him so much . . . !

Lorenzo, you're the one who's a magician.

No, it wouldn't be fair to cheat my son with these pages in which I've only been able to record my failure, with this notebook which is nothing, unless it represents hope, the path toward the other one that's still empty. Lorenzo can't be my witness, either. I don't want to share my harsh journey with anyone; I feel as if this pain, this suffocating, this desperate sensation of always finding myself in the same place, belongs only to me, and I'm the only one who should suffer from it. I don't want to lighten my load or share the weariness of bearing it. Perhaps in my entire life, it's the only thing I can call mine, mine forever. Company and stimulation can't be received or even desired in that profound moment when something unknown is happening inside a man who's trying to express himself. And each word in my notebook represents one of those indescribable moments. If Lorenzo read this one day, could he understand it? Could he see in it everything I don't say and all of the pain that not being able to say it causes me? It's empty; I know full well it says nothing. But I, and only I, know that this void is full of myself. I can't explain it any other way, and it's impossible to demand or expect someone to listen to what I've never been able to say, no matter how hard I've tried.

No, I can't leave Lorenzo this useless notebook, all of this nothingness. An insignificant event was enough to convince me that it's not possible. It made me understand that an event, a question, a meditation can modify what we supposed were firm conclusions, and the only truth is the one that's made up of all of those we come to during our lives. In other words, nothing is stable, nothing stands motionless in man's trembling heart.

THESE ARE HOPELESS MOMENTS. THESE MO-
ments when I ask myself: can it really be true that I can't write
anything, anything at all? I've already accepted the fact that I
can't find a general theme or sketch the contours of a more-or-
less complete story. But this is too much, having nothing to
say, when for hours I've been anxiously waiting for the time
when I'm free to write. How can I cure myself of this obsession that is more firmly rooted, more vehement, every day, and
every night more of a failure?

My wife's been sleeping peacefully for a while now. She did
everything she set out to do today. What she has to do tomorrow belongs to tomorrow and will also get done.

Our neighbors have turned out the lights in their rooms. I
know them all, they have their problems, some serious. But
they sleep. Right now, I don't have any problems. Lorenzo's
been doing better these last few months, my wife's performing
miracles with our budget, my job's secure. I could sleep peacefully and assign to each day the tasks that belong to it. Why do
I always go to bed with the feeling that it's not time yet, that
something's missing, that in the morning I'll have something
inside me, left over from what I didn't finish the day before? If,
as often happens to me, I stop writing for several nights, because I'm worn out or sleepy, because someone comes to visit,
because of any unexpected circumstances, I feel the same as
when I haven't been able to pay a debt on time and the credi-

tors bang incessantly on the door wanting to collect. On those occasions, at least I can find some pretext or ask for an extension. But with this writing business, who obligates me, to whom am I accountable, to whom am I committed? Not even to myself, because I've never been happy about doing it. I'd understand it if I were like those artists who always know and feel, wherever they may be, that, more than anything else, they have both the obligation and the pleasure of expressing themselves. But I'm not an artist. If I really were, I'd have a certainty within me even though, perhaps out of modesty, I wouldn't show it. My wife, my children, my job wouldn't be the center of my life but only the contour, a hazy profile, instead of this rigid, unalterable frame. The artist's a being who's different, wounded for life since birth, who finds it hard to be a part of the day-to-day reality. Of course, there are some who extract the best elements from that reality. But noticing it well enough to give it form and transform it into a work of art is the best proof that they haven't been able to become part of that reality themselves, that they haven't been swallowed up by it. They describe it with such perfection that it's as if they'd broken off a piece of it. What's different about it is what only the great artists achieve: a reality we have always *known* about and, nevertheless, *notice* for the first time.

Right now I understand perfectly that a person obsessed by the need of doing something specific, who's also a prisoner of work obligations and of a family, may decide to give it all up forever. I'm so fed up and worn out by this stupid life! I've neither the time nor the peace of mind to do anything different. I go insane trapped in between so many exact days cut to fit a mold. Every time Rafael Acosta, who has a desk calendar, rips off the page belonging to the day's date, I feel as if he's ripping out a piece of my own life. One more day of work, one day less to live. So much the better. Sometimes I wish I could die so that I won't see how my office mate rips off that calendar page.

Then I think that even if I don't see it, the act will be repeated one day and another and another, and that the important thing isn't me, but the act itself, and the fact that there will always be a prisoner to carry it out.

If I could go away, far away! If I could only do it! One of these evenings, I'll announce that I'm going out for a bit and never come back. Or better still, so that they can't come looking for me, I'll leave a letter in which I explain my indisputable need for seclusion in order to dedicate myself completely to writing an important book. I'll beg my wife to understand, to forgive me, to explain it all to my sons and not to try to stop me. . . .

I'm going away. I'm free. I've been careful enough to leave behind my identification cards, my watch, and the photos I always carry in my wallet. Barely having left my neighborhood where everyone knows me, I can become another man, if I want to: give a false name in hotels and hear myself called Mister Rodríguez, or Mister López instead of that worn-out Mister García. It may seem to be the same thing, and make no difference whatsoever, but for me it does. I've got the urge to show off new things: a new name, corduroy pants, an unknown woman, a bar, a knotted cane, a solitary beach by a gloomy, ferocious sea.

Yes, I'd settle down in a small port, in a very modest house close to the beach where I could hear the sea. I'd just need a bed, a chair, and a huge table. I'd buy twelve thick notebooks, but before locking myself up to write, I'd wander around for a week with no fixed destination, without being in a rush, getting used to my freedom. I'd spend the evenings on the beach watching the sea, the heavens, the broad horizon; I'd sink my hands into the moist sand, I'd swim naked in the rough, black, midnight sea. In the mornings, I'd help the fishermen cast out their nets and then stretch them out in the sun and separate the fish according to size. During the parched afternoons, I'd go to the bar for a drink with the fishermen, and we'd talk. Doubtless, they'd ask me if I were going to stay there and what my trade was. And for the first time in my life, I'd answer out loud, loud enough for everybody to hear: "I'm a writer. I'm writing a book, and I need peace and quiet. I'm going to stay here until I finish it."

Their expression would change immediately. They'd look at me with respect and feel flattered that I'd chosen their far-off, forgotten port. Perhaps one of them would say it on everybody's behalf. I'd buy a bottle, and we'd all drink a toast to my book.

Finally, I lock myself up to write. That first evening in my new house, I sleep deeply, worn out by a week of freedom and forgetting. I wake up quite late in the morning, open my eyes, and look all around me. Am I dreaming? In a few minutes I'll probably hear: "Dear, it's getting late."

I feel something like a tap on my chest. Suddenly, my mind puts everything in order. No, never again will it get late. I'm the master of my time, I'm my own master. I'll get up and just have to walk a few steps to sit down at the table where my twelve new notebooks are waiting for me. No one will interrupt me. If I want to, I can write all day long or two or three days in a row. When I get tired, I'll go to the beach and spend the whole evening stretched out in the sand. Or I'll go to the bar with my fishermen friends, who, when they see me, will ask about my book with great interest.

I have to realize that I'm a free man, a man without a watch, without a calendar, without limitations. I can do as I please. Who's going to stop me? Not my wife, who's so far away and at this very minute—I wonder what time it is?—is probably making lunch for the boys. A very simple lunch, since she doesn't have to make me happy. She probably made rice and eggs . . . , no, no, they aren't good for Lorenzo. Well, she can do as she pleases; I'm not going to worry about those minor details. My wife's strong and has always taken care of everything. She'll find some way to keep the house going. Besides, José can help out; lots of boys put themselves through school. True, my boy isn't very responsible and, if he starts to make money at an early age, he'll surely lose interest in his career. I'd have to avoid this somehow, because I don't want to feel guilty if José doesn't prepare himself properly for life's struggles. Perhaps I could write a few articles or stories for small-town newspapers that aren't very demanding, or give math classes to the port's children, or something else that would give me a modest monthly income. By using Pepe Varela as a middleman and asking him not to mention where I sent the money from, I'd see that my wife got some money to help her out. Of course, it wouldn't amount to much. And what if, in spite of her efforts, she couldn't come up with anything? She's a good housewife, but nothing more. She'd have to get a job as a hotel or nursing-home manager. But then she'd be away from home for most of the day. And what if Lorenzo got sick? He usually comes home nervous after school; he doesn't adapt easily to the company of other children; it's hard for him to pay attention in his classes, and that wears him out and gets him all worked up. He'd find he was all alone, become more melancholy. I've noticed—or maybe it's because I love him so much and we understand each other so well— that when I come home he blushes. He doesn't say anything. He waits for me to greet his mother, take off my jacket, put on my slippers, and wash my hands. He keeps doing whatever he's doing or he follows me at a distance. When he thinks it's the right moment, he comes up to me. He knows I'm going to rub him on the chin or lift him up to my head to kiss him and ask him the same thing: "Did you finish your homework?"

And I know he'll always give me the same answer: "Just have to do my addition."

Or his subtraction, or his multiplication. Since he knows I

work with numbers, he's decided that I should do his math
homework for him. And, surely, to bring me closer to him and
feel that I'm spending part of my time exclusively with him, he
shrewdly pretends to be incredibly stupid. I pretend to believe
him and scold him: "stick-head," "donkey-butt," "pea-brain,"
"rock-head." And he dies laughing.

I CAN'T GO ON. I DON'T WANT TO THINK ABOUT
these things right now. On the contrary, I have to forget about
them. If I could go away someday, be free and live alone. I'd
have to write without stopping, until I started to fall to pieces,
until I felt my head exploding. That's the only way I'd be able
to scare the memories away and put up with the isolation. I
like to imagine I'm free, but at the same time, just by imagining it, something breaks apart inside me. I'm so tied, so tightly
bound to my wife and children, that I can't feel my own boundaries anymore. It's true that a man has his own life, his own destiny, and his own solitude. One day that will vanish, and he'll
join his wife and children to tie that tight knot I'm feeling
right now. But that knot can only be undone by something
natural, by something inexorable, like instinct and death.

I write this complete thought and think that if an artist read
it, he'd tell me that art is as natural and inexorable as instinct
and death. How could I answer him? I, who am not a true artist, who only feel this overwhelming need to write, have been
imagining for several hours now how I could abandon my family and bury myself forever in my notebooks. How could I re-
fute the argument of a person for whom art is life and death
itself? No, I couldn't do it. I might tell him that art, life, and
death are man himself and his relationship with others, and
that the artist is he who is born with all of man's signs plus one
that distinguishes and compels him. Some will give extreme
preponderance to that single sign, painfully mutilate the others,

choose solitude, and surrender themselves entirely to it. Others will find a space and an expression of that sign in the center of their lives. Still others won't be able to save it and will see it drowned in the circumstances of a harsh, gloomy existence. And still others will only feel it inside them like a strange anxiety and won't know how to recognize it.

What can I say for myself? Nothing. I don't know. I don't know what's wrong with me. But right now, after having imagined the freedom that might allow me to write (which is a way of expressing myself, but which would also keep me from living my daily, intimate reality, another essential form of expression), I know that before becoming a writer—supposing that I ever do—I'll be what I have been and always will be: a man who needs to write and live imprisoned in his natural and unchangeable cell.

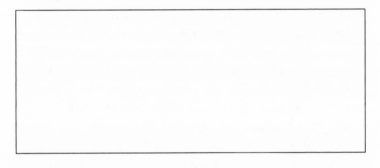

I HAVE TO STOP SMOKING SO MUCH OR TRY TO sleep a little more. I'm losing my memory, becoming distracted, and every day my job seems more demanding. Simply abandoning my notebook for a week or two makes me forget what I've written. Everything is becoming disjointed and anarchic.

I say this because a few nights ago I felt ashamed while I was rereading some pages, those in which I formally promise not to write for six months. Later, as if I had never made any such commitment, I started to talk about my children and then re-tell past events, which are now so far-off that they can't justify breaking my formal promise. And it's really because I forgot. I don't know if I brought up that relationship between José and Margarita deliberately, so that the act of writing would seem like an interest in my sons and not a need to keep writing. Then, giving in to enjoyable temptation, I told that long story about Lupe Robles, which was really painful when I reread it.

I don't know, but while I was writing it, and even though somewhere I might say the opposite, I felt totally detached from the main character. But when I read it, I felt that all of that had happened to me, that I was the one who had stayed with her for two years and the one who had deeply suffered her absence. Above all, I felt that that woman still existed and, in reality, I hadn't completely forgotten her.

That's the only way I can explain the vehement desire to see her that suddenly welled up in me, and I even thought of going to look for her. But before going, and this kept me from doing it, I played around a little with the idea and imagined the scene.

Only three years have gone by since I left her. Of course, in three years a lot of things happen to a person, but since so few things have happened to me in fifty-six, it's natural for me to suppose that in three, nobody's life is going to change drastically.

I thought she'd be carrying on as usual and that it'd be easy to go to her house, ring the bell twice, as was my custom, and listen to the clicking of the uncomfortable high heels she'd wear all day long. I thought that while I heard it, and until the door opened, my heart would beat fast, and the minute we were face to face she'd notice I had become very pale.

Everything up to that point was easy for me to imagine, but later, curiously enough, I couldn't go on with the game. I know very well what my wife would say if I were to come back after three years of absence, no matter what the reason might have been for it: "Thank God!"

I'd walk into my house, and everything else would come about naturally, all by itself.

On the other hand, I can't know, or even imagine, what Lupe would say if I came back after such a long time. It's just as possible that she'd throw herself on my neck in an exaggerated display of happiness. Or she might hurl an insolent, "What in the hell are *you* doing here?!" Anything is possible. And it's not that the welcome would be the result of her true feelings, or of the emotions tied to the particular moment, but instead of her current situation. If she had another man, she'd receive me with arrogance and confidence; if she didn't have another man, with jubilation and great emotion.

This lack of orientation, this inability to choose and define the limits of the elements that would work in the scene of a return, this inability to lean toward either frank drama, or restrained emotion, or open frivolity, kept me from playing with the idea and, therefore, from holding on to it. It was watered down with other meditations, and I'm not going to torment myself anymore. That's over and done with.

My life is flowing along peacefully. I shake it up sometimes, artificially, with this battle between writing and not writing. On occasion, I think that my writing comes from its being the only tool I have to make sure I don't forget about myself completely; that perhaps the object of my insistence on recording the most important events in my life has been reconciling myself with my life and discovering that it hasn't been so mediocre.

Because it's true I haven't triumphed in anything, I've never been an important man or enjoyed prosperity, I've never committed a single heroic act or been recognized in any newspaper, either for anything good or anything bad, for that matter; no one would consider me for a position of higher responsibility or for political office; nor would it ever occur to anyone to propose that I take part in a criminal act or even a cover-up. In the end, my name will never stand out. It is destined to appear, with peaceful regularity, only on an employees' payroll. That's what's called, without extenuating circumstances, being mediocre.

And, well, I accept it. What I want to say is that sometimes, deep inside me, and I don't know if it's only to console myself, I feel that the mediocre man can also triumph, if by triumph we understand not just dazzling appearance, fame, or prosperity, but inner peace without the desire to pursue those flashy elements that give a sumptuous contour to existence. I'm referring to the average man who knows he's average and accepts his stature with humility. I've met some, and it seems to me they live with great dignity and ease.

But this conclusion is useless for me. I don't accept my stature humbly. Deep down, I'm always scorning it or substituting for it another, laden with remarkable features. This often happens to me with an almost alarming frequency, I could say. More clearly, more sincerely: I like to play the part of the hero. And to do it, I use many varied circumstances. The end result is the same as little Lorenzo achieves more cleanly and directly when he puts three feathers on his head and, convinced of his transformation, emphatically shouts: "I'm an Indian warrior!"

It's all the same. But I, a poor adult, have to resort to other methods to create my characters. For example, I've already said that I'm very susceptible to the flu; it hits me with a vengeance and gives me a fever for two or three days. So when it's already late at night, and I'm suffering from it, my head aches and my eyes are sore, I think of telling my wife: "I'm going to my office. I want to write for a while."

I already know what she'll say: "What you need right now is to sleep, instead of going into that freezing room to waste your time."

Hearing her automatically sets up the situation I want: I argue, she tries to make me see reason; I get stubborn, I win, I go into the room, lock the door, and the game begins inside me. I'm a misunderstood artist who, overcoming all obstacles, comes to his notebook with a heroic spirit.

Naturally, I can't start writing immediately. Then I concentrate and imagine miserable conditions, dramatic circumstances, or rather melodramatic circumstances: I'm deathly ill, I live in a cold attic in an old Paris neighborhood, I have to struggle fiercely against hostility and poverty to write a book that will one day be famous . . . .

All this to maintain my heroic spirit that, moment by moment, within my true surroundings, is leaving me farther and farther behind.

A few minutes go by. I try to begin. I can't, that's the truth. My wife was right. I'm freezing in this damned room, my head aches terribly, my eyes are burning, and all I really want is to get into the bed her body has surely already warmed up. Only one thought stops me: that she's still awake and will receive me, maternally embrace me to warm me up, and at the same time will assail me with her pitiless reasoning: "I knew you wouldn't be able to stay in there. But you always have to have your way. . . ."

I still try to defend myself a little: "You don't understand . . . !"

"What I understand is that you're sick and you'll wake up worse. Cover yourself up well and try to get some sleep."

And so, our two worn-out and discolored blankets and her cutting but loving remark make the beautiful game of the misunderstood artist disappear. What he really needs is sleep.

I don't know. It's a kind of obsession. Or maybe it's the need to transform things as well as to transform myself. I know it's ridiculous to talk about this, but sometimes, when I'm in the shower, the thick stream of water that pounds on my face makes me think of gales and angry seas. My imagination takes things to the point that I forget I'm a clerk who has to arrive at a certain time, who only has a few minutes to take a shower, and I trade places with an intrepid captain at the helm of his ship, who, with great skill and daring, manages to save it from the furious assault of the waves. All these dreams of absurd exploits make me stay in the bathroom longer than usual.

Suddenly, the game is broken up by my wife's voice, hurrying me along: "Are you going to spend the whole day in there? You'll be late."

I'd rather not mention how embarrassed I feel when this happens and I abruptly return to the reality of our chipped tub, the rusty shower pipe, my towel that still shows what's left of that huge initial my wife embroidered, and above all, my feeble body, incapable of any exploit whatsoever.

At the office, I manage to control such foolishness. True, the surroundings aren't very conducive and, besides, any poorly done calculations that I don't notice can cost me money or long hours of additional work. But at home or in the street, the slightest incident helps me to escape for a little while. If one of my legs hurts and I lean to take the weight off it and reduce the aching, I close my eyes and think that it's riddled with bullet wounds I got in the campaign when I boldly saved the lives of several comrades. Now I'm suffering in a hospital; my family has no idea where I am, perhaps I'll die, but some day my exploit will be recognized, and they'll say: "Whoever would've thought it! He seemed incapable of such a thing!"

One afternoon, two or three weeks ago, I was lying on the couch, daydreaming, playing the hero. Suddenly my wife asked: "What are you thinking about?"

"Nothing."

"That's not true. I saw it in your face . . . tell me!"

I never should have trusted her: at that moment, risking my own life, I had just saved two children from the flames.

My wife laughed: "And didn't you think of your own children, who might've ended up as orphans?"

I told her everything: They didn't exist. I had just escaped from prison. I had been locked up in a dungeon for two years for political reasons. I was the leader of a rebel band that had challenged the tyrant.

"But José, aren't you ashamed . . . at your age?"

"Yes."

"You're worse than Lorenzo."

"That's right."

Just to have something to say, I asked her if she ever had fantasies.

"Sometimes. But always about things that can become true."

Now I was really interested in her answer!

"And you think I could never save two children from the flames or be persecuted for my political ideals?"

"No, darling. You're over the hill."

I deduced that, had I not been over the hill, she would've considered me capable of exploits of that sort. In other words, I was once capable of it, I could have done it. I never did because there was no opportunity, because time passed me by, but not because I was innately incapable. The best proof of that—I further deduced—was that inside me, that heroic character is still alive, and my imagination is still at the service of his abundant, varied exploits.

I can't do anything to make them reality for that very reason, because time has gone by. Before, when it still hadn't happened, I didn't know it went so quickly, that we don't even feel it, not even later when we begin to notice its passing. But by then it has already gone.

It's really very hard. You end up being trapped by matters of the heart, of instinct, of hope; then by your duties, by the house, by your children. You don't know, you don't sense which is the exact day you should make your mark, or take a bold tack and change your course, in spite of the howling wind.

How was I to know that the sum total of all of those distinct "tomorrows" that had melted together in my mind, tomorrows that had already become "todays" and "yesterdays" without my noticing, would make not only time go by, but my time, the only thing that is mine?

Who's going to keep watch over time and measure its passing between daily events and loving endeavors, between those relentless duties, between sad dates and other anxiously awaited ones, between other dates lost in others and in still others, always the same ones that make up the common man's life?

How was I to think of the transcendence and the perils of time's passing, when one day in February I had exclaimed, as I embraced my wife: "In October, before the baby is born, we're going to move into a big house where there's lots of sunlight!"

Nine months, nine months of my own life that, for me, didn't mean any more than waiting for my son, and the chance to settle him in a large, sunlit house! If I was thinking of time like that then, like an unalterable and estranged concept, it was only to want it to go by quickly.

And later the same thing: hoping it would go by quickly so the child would grow up, go by as quickly as possible so as to accumulate more years of service and have the right to a better salary, go by quickly when my wife suffered so much with her second pregnancy; hoping now that the months will go by quickly so that we'll have paid off the pending debts; that it will go by quickly; go by quickly so that Lorenzo will finally leave behind his many childhood sicknesses.

And so, hoping that time will pass so that the daily problems that weigh us down will also pass, we find one day that our own time has passed.

And, our attic in Paris, our famous book, our ship in the

middle of a gale, our battlefield exploits . . . , our name, all have remained on the threshold, intact and ageless.

We are a bunch of mediocre people. We couldn't prevent it, or we didn't have what it took to prevent it. We weren't blessed with those talents or qualities that can't be stifled. Our own insignificant, common talents, sunk in a sea of time, will never be noticed or talked about.

Some people, perhaps, like myself, realize it and secretly grieve in the pages of a notebook. Still others don't even have the time to notice that their time has already passed. But I'm sure that, without being able to avoid it, thousands of them close their eyes, just the way I do, forget their families, their jobs, their sickness, their age, and, with their imaginations, carry out those magnificent exploits they still believe themselves capable of. Any little thing, a child's cry, the sound of a watch, the sound of a fallen plate, the banging of a door, a familiar voice, any little thing will bring them back to their dense, gray reality. But they will always find new ways to escape, to play the hero's role, and to attend a completely secret ceremony in which only they, along with the others they could have been, pin on their own chests the medal that allows them to glorify their name and break free from the rank and file.

That long, never-ending, uniform line which we can leave only by entering another more anonymous, still more abstract one: the never-ending line of the dead, where we'll be remembered only for a while by four or five relatives who'll live a few years longer than we. After that, no one. Nothing. Not even a thought in passing, not even the slightest trace in a single person's memory. Nothing!

But, can you live, can you die like that?

And the only release, this shameful clandestine notebook (which I once thought could become a book) I write in some evenings when I'm not overwhelmed by those tasks and worries that took my time away from me forever.

IT MUST BE VERY LATE ALREADY BECAUSE MY wife has turned on the light. It's her way of letting me know she's still awake and that I should go to bed. I'm not sleepy. I want to keep writing. Better yet, to start writing because tonight my time's been spent on fantasies, digressions, and memories. That's not the way it really is; I know better. If I could find a strong, precise, impressive first sentence, then maybe the second one would be easier for me, and the third one would come all by itself. The real problem is the beginning, the starting point.

That light, it really gets on my nerves. Anyway, I'm going to go to bed and keep on thinking. I've got to find that first sentence. I've just got to find it.